Saint Nicholas,

the Christmas Story

Matt 6:33

Some of the 5 STAR reviews at Amazon.com...

"The next Christmas Classic!"

★ ★ ★ ★ ★ 5 Stars

"This is one book I will re-read every Christmas. It is a combination of history, fiction, fantasy, fun and education. It's fun to imagine if it could be real, and I had no idea what was coming next. It was very difficult to put down and one book that I enjoyed very much. I highly recommend this book for all ages."

★ ★ ★ ★ ★ 5 Stars

"I found this book when doing my daily check of Amazon's Movers and Shakers list for my Kindle. I got the sample and quickly bought the book. The book starts when a young girl asks her Father, "Is Santa Claus Real?" The story begins and I was immediately drawn in. I could not stop reading! I became vested in the characters and felt as if I knew them. Mr. Eldridge does an excellent job of weaving the history and fiction together. After finishing Saint Nicholas I felt warm and fuzzy and I wanted to do something for someone else. Isn't that part of what Christmas is all about, doing for others? This is a book I plan to read every December. I look forward to Mr. Eldridge's next book."

★ ★ ★ ★ ★ 5 Stars

"I enjoyed this story immensely. I learned more about the historical Saint Nicholas and his life of helping others. And I enjoyed the fantasy of incorporating the current Santa Claus elements into the historical story while emphasizing the true meaning of Christmas. This book read like a suspense story & kept my attention throughout. Great job - I hope to read more books by Matthew Eldridge in the future."

★ ★ ★ ★ ★ 5 Stars

"This was a wonderful book! Once I started reading I couldn't put it down. I loved how Mr. Eldridge combined fact and fiction to make such an interesting book about the story of Santa Claus. This is a great explanation for all the Christmas traditions from the elves and the red suit to the flying reindeer. I plan to add this to my Christmas collection and share it with my own children as well. I highly recommend this great book!"

Saint Nicholas,

the Christmas Story

MATTHEW ELDRIDGE

Published by Matthew Eldridge. 134 Crowell Road S.E. Conyers, GA 30094

meldridge@cheerful.com 770-364-3990

www.mattheweldridge.net

Cover illustration by James W. Elston
 http://www.jameselston.com/

This is a work of historical fiction fantasy. This story is based on the true life of Saint Nicholas (Santa Claus), Bishop of Myra. Some of the characters in this book are taken straight out of history, while others were fictionalized. There was a great amount of research put into this story, and while I tried to stay true to the historical facts, events, characters, and timeline, some things had to be changed or condensed in order to keep the story interesting.

ISBN   145283444X

EAN-13   9781452834443.

Printed in the United States of America

For my children.

Prologue

The young boy sat between his parents, watching them fade. His mother had become delusional, talking to long-lost relatives, who were supposedly standing at the end of her bed. His father wheezed, drowning in congestion, weak, and frail.

It was just weeks before the town would celebrate the Festival of the Christ. Distant family would soon be arriving. But for now, the young lad would have to be the adult and take care of his ailing parents.

The child prayed for what seemed to be an eternity. He prayed with every bead of sweat that poured from his mother's brow. He prayed with every cough that came from his father's lips. He didn't know much about this God he was praying to, but he knew this: nothing he could do on his own would save his parents.

The boy felt his prayers were heard when the local priest stopped by for a visit and anointed his family with oil. Encouraged by his parents, the young boy returned to the orphanage with the man of God. He never saw his parents again. What he experienced the next few years of his life would change the future of the world.

Chapter 1

It was a long winter's day and I was exhausted. I was happy to be home, although I enjoyed every second of the day's journey. I made my way through the narrow, wooden foyer, dropped my keys on a shelf, the wood scratched from the repetitive daily routine, and followed the soothing smell of hot chocolate into the living room.

"Daddy!" Makayla yelled to me, getting up from her place on the living room floor and running to me with open arms. I feared the chocolate mustache that matched her long brown hair, but how could I resist a hug from such an eager child? She was my middle daughter and had just turned four a few weeks before.

Her sisters Gabriella and Elisha soon followed suit, tackling me with their hugs and kisses. Mommy made her way out of the kitchen and brought me a cup of my favorite; hot chocolate mixed with a little coffee and a dash of chili powder.

I plopped down in my favored rocking chair and took a deep breath, staring at the fireplace. The fire painted the room an amber glow while popping, crackling, and whistling a soundtrack to its beauty. The girls were more quiet than usual, and getting along quite well. I assumed it was the excitement of Christmas Eve, but it could have been they were exhausted from playing all day with their cousins Calvin, Jackson, and Parker.

"How'd it go, honey?" my wife called out from the kitchen.

"Good. The roads weren't too bad, either… just a little snow."

"Did you get to see any of the kids?" she asked anxiously.

"A few."

I made our annual family tradition of gathering up presents and taking them to the different ministries such as the women and children's abuse center, the Good Oaks Homes Village for orphans or abandoned children, and the Refuge Center, a homeless shelter for families.

Actually, I was just the delivery driver. My wife took the joy in finding the gifts, separating them into age and gender categories, and then making the stockings or boxes for them. This year she and our girls picked out gifts for more than thirty children. If we could have afforded more, she would have bought more. She has a big heart, and Christmas was her favorite time to flex it. She had encouraged several of her friends to join our adventure, and so I rounded up the mom's group gifts to deliver as well.

We always counted our blessings. At one point both of us were attached to one of these centers, either as an employee, a volunteer, or with family who resided there. We knew the hardships these families faced, and it brought pure joy knowing that we could ease their pain a little.

I took a few more sips of my hot chocolate-coffee blend and thought about the day's events, waiting for Nicole to join us in the living room. God had been good to us. After fourteen years of marriage and several job changes, we finally owned our first home. It wasn't just any house; we loved our quaint, two-story, white and grey four bedroom country home, complete with fireplace. We both felt blessed and guilty at the same time: Blessed that it was ours, guilty because there are so many people without, especially in these hard economic times.

I stared at the Christmas tree, adjacent to the fireplace, standing tall in the corner and adorned with presents almost three feet deep. Its lights glared in my glasses, imitating stars and miniature galaxies glowing on dark green limbs. The brown floor rug covered a portion of the shiny wood flooring, tying the tree to the fireplace. Five little stockings colored in swirls of red, white, and green hung from the fireplace mantle. I stared back at the new wood floors and chuckled at the memories of my own childhood Christmases.

...She stood about eight feet tall. She was full, green, and gorgeous. My father handpicked her from a local tent sale, still alive and filled with sap. He didn't care that the sap ruined his new leather gloves; he was excited that we had a *real* Christmas tree this year.

My mother always convinced my dad to buy an artificial tree because of my childhood asthma. My dad sacrificed a lot because of my illnesses: a son who couldn't mow the lawn, play a lot of sports, or even have a real

Christmas tree in the house. But this year, he and I convinced Mom that if we were truly to celebrate the holiday, then we MUST have a real tree. I was getting older and had fewer and fewer asthma attacks. Besides, I had my trusty inhaler.

Dad fought with the gargantuan tree to get it in our garage. After cutting off some limbs, he battled it again to enter the house. We'd never had a tree so tall, or so wide, come to think of it. He proudly placed the newly-trimmed fir in her stand, and Mom and I took over the decorations.

Florida heat was a killer of the Christmas spirit, so Mom would crank the AC down to about fifty-five degrees and we'd light a fire. Yes, we were blessed—one of the only homes in central Florida to actually own a fireplace. Perhaps it was because our home was built before heaters were invented. Who knows? But in all honesty, I think we only needed it twice in my eighteen years of living there.

I would turn up Dad's stereo, playing all our Christmas favorites while we dressed the tree in non-matching, sometimes gaudy, yet very memorable, ornaments. Oh, and of course there was the string of plastic candy looking like lifesavers that I would chew on as a child. And I can't forget the glass gingerbread man that I bit the ear off during my toddler years. It definitely looked better than it tasted. Mom always hung it from the tree, ear missing and all, so that our relatives could relive the comical experience year after year.

The memories of obnoxious, enormous colored light bulbs infesting our 1970's Christmas trees make me cringe. But there was never any tinsel on our tree. Never. Tinsel was the enemy. Why, to this day, I still don't know. Every year I would ask for it, and every year I'd get the same firm answer.

I'd understand if we had pets, like my wife's family for example. She has vivid memories of her cats running around the house at Christmas time with tinsel hanging out of their butts after swallowing it days before. I wouldn't believe it had I not witnessed it myself when we started dating.

Finally, the tree was dressed in all her splendor, and Dad would hold me high to put the angel on the very top. This special year, I remember Dad lifting me, stretching as high as he could so that I could reach the tip of this mammoth pine. S-T-R-E-T-C-H. I was almost there...

CRASH! The tree fell down, ornaments shaken or broken against the hard wood floor. Dad put it back up. We rearranged the ornaments and threw away the broken ones. Of course Dad found a few that we missed when he stepped on them with his bare feet.

The next day Dad, Mom, and I came home to the tree lying on the floor of the living room again. Dad realized the stand might be too small, so he went out and purchased another one.

The following day we came home to a horizontal tree in our living room with a tenth of the ornaments gracing the floor.

Dad always made our Christmases special. In fact, I think he overdid it. I can't remember a Christmas where I didn't get almost everything I ever wanted. Notice I said "almost." I still haven't gotten that drum set I asked for every year from age six to seventeen.

Dad definitely made this year unique. In fact, it quickly became the most memorable Christmas we've ever had. Each year as the family gathers, one of us reminds him of his craziest Christmas stunt.

Mom and I had been shopping for Dad's Christmas gift that year at the local mall and upon making our way into the driveway, saw that Dad had beaten us home. That's not all he was beating.

Thwack! Thwack! Thwack!

Then we heard him angrily mumbling some words that we couldn't understand through the door. Mom was brave enough to enter the house and witness Dad firsthand as he lifted his hammer and...

Thwack!

"Chipper! What are you doing?" she yelled, appalled.

She ran over to him, watching in horror as my Dad pierced her brand-new wood floors with thick, silver nails.

"You nailed the Christmas tree to the floor! Are you crazy?"

"It won't fall again!" my dad triumphed, very sure of himself.

Gabriella, my affection-hungry five year old, climbed into my lap and smothered me in kisses. She placed her head on my shoulder, a sure way to melt my heart, and proceeded to ask me a question.

"Daddy?"

"Yes, sweetheart?"

"Is Santa Claus real?"

OH MY GOSH! My heart almost stopped beating. She's too young to be asking me these questions, I thought to myself.

My palms began sweating and I became uncomfortably warm. How do I answer this?

"Yes dear, he's very real."

"Today Allison said her Daddy was really Santa Claus."

I took a sip of my hot chocolate, buying time to scrounge up an answer.

"Maybe he pretended to be Santa Claus at a school or something, kind of like your Poppa does for the kids in Nana's kindergarten class?"

I could tell she was deep in thought, contemplating what I said.

"Ms. Charlene had a picture of him with her when she was little, but he didn't look like Santa at the mall."

"Can I tell you a secret?" I whispered to her.

She leaned her head back and locked her big brown eyes with mine. I leaned forward.

"No one we know has ever seen Santa Claus. Santa's really too busy to go to the mall or visit with people except on Christmas. Those are his helpers. They work for Santa. He won't let people see him."

"Why?"

"I don't know. Preparing for Christmas, I guess."

Gabriella took a few breaths and thought about her next question. "So what does he look like?" she asked.

"He's not like people describe him. But he's definitely a real person."

"Does he wear a red suit?"

"Yup," I said with a smile.

Gabriella thought about it for a minute. "What about the reindeer?"

"What about them?" I said.

"Are they real? Do they fly?"

"Yes, they are very real, and…well, they sort of fly."

"How can he…," she placed her finger on her chin, thinking hard, "…really visit every home in the world in one night?"

"It's called the Spirit of Christmas, Gabby."

"How does he get down the chimney being so fat? Does he use magic?"

"Well…yes, there is something magical about him. But not the type of magic you're thinking of. Besides, honey, I don't really think he is as big as we make him out to be. You can thank Coca Cola for that one."

"Huh?"

"Never mind," I answered sharply, knowing that an open door to a new revelation meant another thirty minutes of investigative questions. I would share about Saint Nick, Coca Cola, and the Great Depression some other time.

Makayla made her way over to me and climbed up on the other side of my lap. She was a tiny little thing, weighing no more than 30 lbs. It was hard to believe that the two older girls were only a year apart. Mom came in the room and picked Elisha up from the floor, and cradled the toddler in her arms.

"Stocking time!" said my beautiful red-headed wife, Nicole, grinning from ear to ear. It was our tradition to open stocking stuffers every Christmas Eve.

She pulled the stockings from the wall and placed them in front of the children. One by one they pulled out their gifts until the stockings were empty. Makayla, always the explorer, reached her hand down deep into the barren stocking and pulled out a shiny penny. The four year old squealed. Gabby and Elisha pulled theirs out too. Makayla remembered it would be there, as it was an annual tradition started by my father twenty-something years earlier.

I expected Gabby to ask me the story of the pennies again, as she usually did each year. But instead, her mind was still focused on the truth about Santa Claus. She was a gifted child, and this "gift" often brought about thorough thoughts and questions, examinations and investigations of every minute detail of every subject of interest, forcing her Mom and I to stay on our toes at all times.

"Daddy, tell me everything you know about Santa Claus."

"Hmm," I sighed. We started rocking in my favorite chair again, the same chair that my dad would rock me in almost thirty years earlier, just before he'd tell me the true story of Santa Claus.

"After dinner?" I queried.

"No. Now!"

I pleaded with the five year old, "But it's a long story."

"You can finish it after dinner," Gabby suggested with a smile.

"Your Mimi's coming in the morning. You need to get some sleep tonight. Are you sure you want me to start it?"

"Yes!" both girls yelled, one on each knee.

"Let's see…"

Chapter 2

Around 300 A.D.

It was a cold, wintry night, colder than usual for the city of Patara. More than twenty boys in the monastery's orphanage found their way to the long, wooden dinner table to warm their innards by the hot soup being served. Everyone, that is, except young Johansen.

Johansen was a timid boy between the ages of ten and eleven, just below five feet tall, with blonde hair and blue sapphire eyes. He had recently lost his parents, and getting him to eat had become an impossible task. Sitting on his bed, Johansen stared out the window of the boys' sleeping quarters, gazing into the dark sky. The large bare room held about twenty faded, white cots, aligned in four perfect rows of five each, dressed perfectly like a military barrack. Snow was accumulating on the ground, and frost graced the window, reflecting a portion of Johansen's face.

Nicholas, one of the young monks at Patara, walked up behind Johansen and watched him quietly through the glare. This brought back memories of a time twenty years before.

Young orphaned Nicholas sat at the window, staring out into the blizzard night. He was about the same age as young Johansen. The orphanage den mother, a sweet woman with motherly features, no makeup, weathered skin, and long brown hair wound tightly in a bun, urged Nicholas to eat his porridge dinner.

"They're coming! They promised we'd spend the Festival of the Christ together!" he pleaded, his voice strained with doubt.

Nicholas's thoughts shifted to the following morning. Again, the den mother urged young Nicholas to eat breakfast as she wiped away his tears with her hand. Her eyes were compassionate. She reached out to hug him, searching for words to say, but nothing could take the pain from the abandoned pre-teen.

The words echoed in young Nicholas's mind from the night before:

"They're dead."

"Both of them?" asked the young woman assisting the den mother.

"Yes. It was the plague," the den mother answered, eyes quickly shifting, her hands nervously fondling a sheet to be folded.

Silence.

Whispers of well-meaning women sound like mountaintop shouts in a quiet, bare room. They pretended young Nicholas couldn't hear their conversation, and he pretended right along with them.

Focusing on the present, the now grown Nicholas grasped the wooden cross hanging from his waist and rubbed it a few times. Hanging just above his knee, the cross often swung against his long, brown, winter robe as he walked. He often found himself holding it tightly to keep it from bouncing around. Nicholas placed his hand on Johansen's shoulder and softly rubbed it endearingly.

"Johansen, please come eat your supper," he said gently.

Monks Nicholas, Peter, and Jude sat in Nicholas's beige, humble, clay room after the orphans all went to bed. The room was no bigger than a walk-in closet, and without windows, became less welcoming than a prison cell. There was a worn cot against the wall where Nicholas slept.

All three monks were in their twenties, and very new converts. Nicholas and Jude's faces still boasted baby soft skin, while Peter attempted to grow a thin-line beard, adorning all the empty patches of a boy just out of puberty trying to grow full facial hair for the first time.

"So, are you guys with me?" Nicholas said mischievously.

Monks weren't known as the mischievous type. However, when it came to blessing the lives of others, Nicholas couldn't help himself.

Peter wagged his head. "You're crazy!"

"Hey, isn't this why we're here in the first place? To help people, to touch their lives in Christ, and to devote ourselves to God by helping the less fortunate?" reminded Nicholas, appealing to his friends' consciences.

"Yeah, but I still say you're crazy!"

"Sounds like fun to me!" Jude replied.

Nicholas piped up excitedly, "So you're in, Jude?" His eyes sparkled with the thoughts he was organizing in his mind.

"I didn't say that!" Jude scolded him, not very convincingly.

Peter warned, "If the Bishop finds out, we'll be exported for sure."

"What about the Cardinal?" provoked Jude.

The three young men shuddered at the thought.

It was just past midnight when Peter, Jude, and Nicholas made their way into the boys' room, carrying bags of nuts and tropical fruits foreign to the region. As twenty boys were sawing logs in their cots, Nicholas went from shoe to shoe filling them with the goodies. He also made his way to the fireplace where several pairs of socks were hung to dry, and filled those as well.

As Nicholas approached young Johansen's cot, he had to reach down and pull the small, brown, weathered shoe from under his bed. A sleepy Johansen slowly opened his right blue eye, stretched, yawned, recognized Nicholas, and mumbled, "Is it morning yet?"

"No, Johansen, go back to sleep," the monk quietly responded, rubbing the young man's head.

Too tired for conversation or to question what Nicholas was doing there, Johansen turned over in his cot and Nicholas lovingly helped pull his covers over him.

The girls' orphanage in Patara was part of the same monastery, but separated by the wide, empty dining hall and located down a damp, narrow, winding walkway. The same gift givers would make their way into the girls' room to fill shoes and stockings before the night was over too.

The morning sun made its way across the Mediterranean ocean, up the mountain cliffs, and through the thick trees, before intruding on the uncovered windows of the monastery. To both monks and orphans, it was the wakeup call with its blinding rays attacking anything that tried to stay asleep. As the first yawning boy sat up and noticed the nuts and fruits in his shoes, his yelps of jubilee quickly woke the others. Soon, the entire room was filled with laughter, excitement, and endless joy as each orphan checked his shoes and socks for surprises.

The sun took a little longer to reach the southwest side of the monastery where the girls lived. However, it wasn't long before high pitched giggles and shrieks bounced around the room and echoed the empty hallways.

"I want to know who's responsible for this!" exclaimed Cardinal St. Michaels, exposing his short temper. A self-proclaimed saint, the Cardinal walked the halls with a commanding presence. Bishop Bartholomew, the local bishop of Patara, walked closely behind him.

Cardinal St. Michaels was Cardinal to the previous Emperor, and Cardinal to all monasteries in the South East Asia Minor region. His temporary quarters resided in Patara, the largest and most modern monastery, coincidentally located in the most modern of cities in the southeast. The Cardinal had great influence on the city, and it appeared to have great influence on him as well. He was a contradiction. He breathed tradition and formality, yet was easily enticed by the recognition he received in the modern market place.

"Those children are unruly and out of control! It's important we keep structure, order, and maintain discipline around here if we ever expect these children to amount to anything!" Cardinal St. Michaels turned around and looked at Bishop Bartholomew, his face tendering as he softly requested a positive response. "We're doing a good job, aren't we? The kids are being fed and clothed! We're teaching them discipline and common prayer! It only takes one small event like this to undo everything we've taught them and to lead them to chaos."

Monk Nicholas made his way through the dark, damp winding hallway and into the small office quarters of Cardinal St. Michaels—as requested by Bishop Bartholomew. He could sense fear from Brother Peter as he walked out of the Cardinal's office, his eyes shifting, refusing to meet with Nicholas's. Nicholas hesitated, and then entered.

Cardinal St. Michaels was fumbling with something on his desk when he asked, "I understand that you were responsible for the disruption at the orphanage this morning?"

"Yes Cardinal. It wasn't a disruption. I just wanted…"

The Cardinal sternly looked at Nicholas and interrupted, "Do you understand that such unruly events can have catastrophic results? We are here to teach discipline, structure, and tradition. We have chosen a vow of poverty for the sake of our God, and we don't want to teach our young children opposite values from our own." His words sounded mechanical and forced.

"Yes, Cardinal, we chose poverty. The children did not," a meekly Nicholas answered.

"Did you? Did you choose poverty? Where'd you get the foreign fruits and nuts? Did you steal them? Take a bribe? Hmmm?" The Cardinal folded his hands, satisfied with the accusation towards his brother in the Lord.

Nicholas lowered his head, resisting the urge to defend himself.

"Consider yourself on probation. You will remove yourself from educating the orphans and will find satisfactory work in the kitchen for the next six weeks."

Nicholas replied with desperation, "But Cardinal, those kids need me. They…"

"They need discipline, order, and structure!" interrupted the Cardinal, standing up with an air of finality and judgment.

Nicholas held the stone bowl with one hand while pouring vegetable stew into it with the other. He repeated this task until enough bowls were filled for the orphans' evening meal.

Patricia, a sixteen-year-old lanky orphan girl, was helping Nicholas deliver soup to the youth.

"Brother Nicholas, did you hear about our morning?"

"Yes. Did you enjoy it?"

"Oh, yes! It was the best morning ever! We couldn't wait to tell you!" gushed Patricia, as she took two more bowls of soup and headed out of the kitchen.

Nicholas had a way with children. He loved them, and they loved him back. He connected well with them. He was the big boy who never grew up. It was as if God himself gave him sips from the fountain of youth. It reflected in his childlike smile, innocent eyes, and ageless, smooth skin. His prayer times were more about God's healing, blessing, and joyfulness in the lives of the youth than about obedience and longsuffering, with the latter being the common prayers of a monk. Perhaps Nicholas saw a side of God that very few did. Perhaps, being robbed of his own childhood made him want to live it through others. Perhaps God had a plan in all of this.

Chapter 3

It was barely conceivable that almost a year had passed since the Festival of the Christ. The trees were almost bare, the sun hid her face again, and the sky breathed a cold chill to those walking in the late afternoon marketplace. Brother Nicholas and Brother Peter kept warm in their brown winter robes as they walked the dirt streets, stopping at a fruit stand where the salesman was packing up his cart. Nicholas picked up a peach and observed it.

"Aren't you the one?" the scraggly looking fruit salesman said with a scratchy voice, as he eyed Nicholas closely.

"The one?"

"Yes, the one who gave fruits and nuts to the street orphans last year at the monastery?"

"No…no…" Nicholas tried to deflect the glory.

"Yeah, you're him! My brother told me about you!" the tall, thin fruit salesman said eagerly, making his way from behind the fruit stand and grabbing hold of Nicholas's arm. "Come here." He took Nicholas to his pile of unsold, miss-matched fruit. "I'm leaving in the morning and I can't take all of this with me. It will spoil. I want you to have it!" The man began to twirl his thick black mustache.

Nicholas smiled. "What do you want me to do with it?"

"Listen, there's a huge storm coming. A lot of us are leaving in the morning for another city, somewhere warmer," he joked, "and we can't take it all with us. I'll tell you what. Let me talk to the market and see what else I can get for you. Do you want me to have it delivered to the monastery?" The man's eyes twinkled.

Nicholas cast a quick glance at Peter.

"Um, no… We'll send someone to get it! Thank you for your kindness," interjected Peter. *There's no turning back*, his spirit sensed, realizing that his answer volunteered his assistance.

The dripping candle appeared to have been burning for hours. The Cardinal didn't notice. His frustrations turned to Bishop Bartholomew who sat across from him in the dim, dreary office.

"…I want his room heavily guarded tomorrow night. I don't know if we can trust him. The children are already talking about what happened last year. They expect it again," said the Cardinal in a deep, brooding voice.

"What do you suggest we do?" replied a weary bishop.

"Find a monk desperate for promotion, and hire him as a guard, pretending to be Nicholas's friend or something. I don't know. Be creative. This is your monastery after all. You need to protect it."

It was the eve of the Festival of the Christ, and the sounds of children's laughter echoed in the empty and often solemn hallways. The room was alive with expectation while the orphans ate their final meal of the day.

Cardinal St. Michaels found his way into the dining hall and stood at the end of the table. It took just seconds for the youth to feel his presence and hush their jubilee. The orphans exchanged knowing glances as he cleared his throat.

"There will be no talk of what happened here last year at this time! There will be no talk of fruits, nuts, or shoes or socks during the Festival of the Christ. We will observe this holiday with humility and propriety. If I hear otherwise, you will be disciplined. Do I make myself clear?"

Although not a single peep was spoken by the children in response, it was obvious by their eyes and tense forms huddled over their bowls that the Cardinal was heard, understood, and feared.

The children were soon stuffed and had tucked themselves into bed with anticipation and hopefulness. The weary kitchen was filled with neglected, dirty stone bowls waiting to be washed, and a floor needing to be mopped. Brother Nicholas dipped his mop into the bucket of murky water and began to scrub the floor. Left to right. Left to right. His left hand held the top of the mop to guide it as his right hand pushed from the middle of the stick. The stone floor seemed to scoff at his efforts. He leaned on the mop for a moment to catch his breath.

Den mother Sarah made her way into the kitchen after tucking the last group of girls in bed. She was a gentle spirit with soft eyes, smooth olive skin, and dark, long hair that she never let down. She didn't look a day over twenty-five. Despite her youthful appearance, it was obvious that she had maturity beyond her years, and that her motherly instincts took over, as she loved on each and every orphan at the monastery.

"There are some excited little children around here who can't go to sleep," she winked with a smile… "It seems someone stirred up a mess that pressed into their little memories for a year now."

Nicholas bowed his head in humility and began mopping again.

"I think that what you did was a wonderful thing. These kids will remember your kindness for the rest of their lives," she spoke softly; leaning into him, close enough that her breath caressed his ear. "If I've ever seen joy in any of them, it was last year, a year ago from tomorrow."

The mop continued to paint the floor with bubbles and wet gloss. Sarah backed off and stood against the counter, watching him as she spoke in a more serious tone. "Listen, I have three girls; all sisters, the oldest who will be of age next month. The orphanage will throw her out after that, and I'm sure the other two will follow. They have a chance to be wed, and cared for, but nothing for a dowry. I don't want to see them end up on these streets as prostitutes."

Swallowing a lump in her throat, Sarah grabbed Nicholas's hand and forced him to look into her soft, large, chocolate eyes. "If you can help them, I'll do what I can to help you."

Brother Jude had just made his way through the hallway and into the dining hall, peeking into the kitchen as Sister Sarah gently leaned up against Nicholas and kissed his cheek—her token of trust and admiration for what Nicholas would do for her girls.

The candle flickered just enough narrow light for Nicholas to read his Bible as he sat in the corner of his small room.

Peter quickly entered. "Nicholas, you can't go anywhere tonight! The Cardinal has people watching you!"

"I can't let those children down!"

"Then I'll go for you! Tell me what to do and I'll do it!" he begged.

"You'd really risk yourself for me?"

"No, for the children!" exclaimed Peter.

"Alright," Nicholas said, as he gathered his thoughts in a military pattern—reparing his war plan, standing up and marching around the miniature room as if he were to conquer it. "The butcher hid his sled down the street near the alley with the surplus on it under a large blanket. After delivering two boxes to the back door of the monastery kitchen, bring the rest on the road to Myra, where a man named Paul will meet you."

"Man, you really got this whole thing figured out, don't you? Why am I meeting him?"

"Because he's going to take the goods to the rest of the orphanages in that area," said Nicholas.

Peter piped up, "Are you crazy? That's like a day's walk one way! Besides, it's freezing tonight."

"Hey, you said you wanted to help, didn't you? Don't worry— you'll be back by morning."

Peter rolled his eyes.

"Well, you better get started," Nicholas spoke in a humorous tone as he sat down again.

Peter quickly glanced down the hallway and back at Nicholas. "Who's going to distribute the gifts here? You can't leave your room."

"Don't worry about me. I have more help than I need."

"Then why am *I* doing this?"

Whispers filled the room as the boys barely contained themselves on their cots. Little ones wished for sweet sleep so that the rising sun would quickly come, peeking her head into their room once again to reveal the gifts of the gift-giver. Each little heart pattered in excitement, with a cadence so fast that slumber was impossible. The whispers turned to hushing and quickly evolved into silence as Cardinal St. Michaels' presence was felt.

The boys were very still as the Cardinal inspected each face, walking gently, slowly by each bed, like a lion searching for its prey.

One of the youngest orphan boys leaned over the edge of his cot and slowly pushed his small, black, worn shoe a little more under him.

Myra was a small town located off the Mediterranean coast. She was sandwiched between the cliffs above the beautiful ocean and the mountains to her northwest, which almost touched one another. Her monastery nestled on the edge of the cliffs in the developing community. It rarely snowed in Myra. This year was the exception. Record snow blanketed the ground in most of Asia Minor, and reached the edges of the coastline from the west.

The path from Patara took travelers through the snowy trees and forests, unless they chose to walk down the cliffs and go around the forest, following the southern coastline. During the summer this was a beautiful journey. However, during the winter, the freezing onshore wind blew against the water and penetrated the clothes and flesh of anyone who dared travel that way. Although the cities were close, the rocky terrain made it an arduous journey.

Peter uncovered the massive sled and revealed the blessings from the marketers; fruits, nuts, clothes, material, meats, vegetables, and a few homemade wooden toys. After dropping off a few boxes at the back door of the kitchen, he recovered the rest of the surplus and began his journey to Myra. The snowfall thickened as the monastery dissolved into the background. Peter pulled his coat tighter around him and covered his face. He could barely see in front of him. The moon diminished along with its light and the road was painted a frosty grey.

Humoring himself and God, Peter cried out, "It only snows like this once every ten years, and it would have to be tonight! A little help here, please?" Peter glanced up to Heaven.

In the distance, Peter saw a small, glowing light. At first, he didn't know if it was real, or if he was seeing an illusion. What would a light be doing in the middle of the roads on a late night, he thought? The bare tree branches stretched like long, boney fingers over the road. Peter didn't let it bother him. "Just keep looking at the light," he told himself.

As Peter approached the amber glow, he noticed a slender figure silhouetted by the candle the man was holding. His thoughts disbelieved, "Could all of that light come from that tiny candle?"

Peter reached the tall, thin, white bearded man, who was wearing a cream colored robe made of thick wool. "Hello, my friend," the man said. "Come inside and have something to drink."

"Are you Paul?" asked Peter, noticing a small hut off the side of the path.

"No, no…"

"I really need to get these supplies to a man named Paul," blurted an anxious Peter, looking around as if he was expecting someone else to come along.

"Don't worry. The children will get their gifts in plenty of time. I'll make sure Paul gets them. Now come inside before you freeze to death. You'll never make it through this storm," replied the insightful, white bearded man.

"How do you know about the children and the gifts?" questioned Peter.

The wise man just smiled.

Peter glanced around the eerie forest one more time before following the man into his makeshift home.

The hut was small, with barely enough room for Peter and his new friend. The inside glowed from the half melted candle in the center of the room. Peter sat on the floor, his legs crossed with his knees pointed up, his arms resting on them. He continued to look to the door, uneasy and unsure. The thin old man placed a warm mug in Peter's hand.

"Try this."

"Mmmmmm... This is good... What is it?" Peter asked, taking a sip of the rich, thick, dark brown drink which clung to his upper lip.

"It's a special recipe. It warms the bones and cleanses the soul. A little bit of cocoa, a little bit of peppermint, with a dash of chili, and my own special ingredient," the man replied with a wink, mixing his own drink with a spoon. He sat down in front of Peter on the other side of the candle. His eyes were twinkling, and his mouth cocked a smile as if he knew something Peter didn't.

"What are you doing way out here in the middle of nowhere?" asked a perplexed Peter.

"Whatever the good Lord tells me to do, and right now, it's making sure you are taken care of." His words trailed off as he lingered on a long sip of his chocolate, chili-mint masterpiece.

Peter sat back for a minute, holding himself up with his arms behind him. He appeared to be relaxing but felt a little confused. "This drink…it's very good, but it's making me a bit dizzy, though." Peter's eyes played tricks on him as he saw two cups in front of him, then three, then four, until he finally passed out.

Jude ran into Peter's room at the Patara Monastery and shook a slumbering Peter.

"Peter, wake up! Wake up! It's morning! Nicholas did it again!" he trumpeted.

Peter slowly sat up and tried to adjust his eyes. He groggily looked around his bedroom, realizing that morning was upon him, and somehow he mysteriously managed to find his way home.

Nuts, fruits, wooden toys, and clothes…the gifts were beyond the boys' wildest dreams. Laughter and smiles filled the room like a fresh aroma, encompassing a usually somber group of children, disguising the otherwise empty, stale space. The boys darted back and forth, showing their treasures off to one another and comparing them.

Across the monastery in the girls' quarters, the young flowers were just waking up to discover what the Festival of the Christ mystery gift-giver brought them. Squeals, shrieks, giggles, tears and "awwws" swirled around their room and flooded out into the halls.

Hope, Patricia, and Catherine stood and watched, congratulating the younger girls on their gifts. All three of the young women were almost of age and would have to leave the orphanage soon. You would never know they were sisters by appearance. Patricia was a skinny redhead with a shapely face. Catherine had dirty blonde short hair, blue eyes, and was very motherly. Hope, the youngest, was the short, petite, olive-skinned child with unmanageable brown curls. Her quirkiness and imagination were an attraction to the boys on the other side.

They were all breathtakingly beautiful, yet, so innocent, with the older two given the opportunity to wed. However, with nothing for a dowry, the engagement would not exist. It was inevitable that pretty soon all three girls would return to the streets from which they were once saved. The youngest was welcome to stay at the orphanage, but the girls made a pact long ago to never allow themselves to separate again.

Their mother died when the oldest was just twelve. Their father, unable to handle losing his wife and best friend, faced the reality of raising three daughters on his own. He turned to alcohol to ease the pain. Within a couple of years, he became a jobless drunk who could never fit the term "sober" in his lifestyle. Unable to pay his bills, he decided to sell his daughters into prostitution.

One of the local nuns from a nearby convent found the girls and saved them from their first sale, bringing them to the orphanage of the Patara monastery. Since their arrival, all three girls had taken the younger ones under their wings.

Den mother Sarah wove her way through the room of excited little girls and approached Patricia, who was holding a redheaded preschooler in her lap.

"Did you girls check your stockings?" prompted the woman who'd become a surrogate mom to them.

"We didn't get anything, den mother," shrugged Hope, "but that's okay. We're almost women now. We're happy to see the children blessed."

"Are you sure? You better check again!" she spoke with influence, just before walking away.

Catherine reached into her seemingly empty green stocking and felt something hard and flat. She pulled it to the surface to reveal a gold coin, the promise of a dowry. Her eyes became saucers as she could barely speak. "Um, Hope…"

Seeing the gold coin in Catherine's hand, Patricia quickly thrust her hand down her own stocking and pulled out a gold coin. Hope quickly followed suit. Joyful tears flowed from the sisters' eyes as they embraced one another.

Chapter 4

It was hard to believe that such a place existed inside the monastery. Deep beneath the earth's surface, down a spiral of clay stairs below the dining hall were the holdings of solitary confinement. It was supposed to be a place of restitution: a place where one could truly be alone with God, repent, and reconnect. It was the alternative to being permanently removed from God's service as a monk.

Cardinal St. Michaels led the way, with Nicholas behind him. Bishop Bartholomew closely followed.

Nicholas entered the small, bleak, black room that had no windows or entry for light.

The Cardinal spoke his final words before the windowless door was shut. "Here, young Nicholas, you will learn obedience and true poverty over the next six weeks. May the Lord be with you and teach you."

With sadness in his eyes, the Bishop locked the door with the long, skinny key and then handed it to the Cardinal.

The young monk messenger eagerly knocked on the door to the monastery. He was intrigued by its size and ambitiously waited to go inside. Brother Jude greeted the new monk and accepted the letter from his hand.

"Cardinal, we just received this from the Myra Monastery," Jude shared as he approached him in his office.

Jude handed the Cardinal the letter, which read:

Dear Cardinal,

Thank you for your generosity of fruits, nuts, meats, and clothes for our orphans. God bless you and God bless Brother Nicholas!

Sincerely,

Bishop Joses

"Unbelievable. He promotes chaos and rebellion, encourages materialism to our children, and they thank him for it!" the Cardinal yelled angrily, before tearing the letter in tiny pieces.

6 weeks later.

Bishop Bartholomew made the long journey down the clay spiral staircase to the room where young Nicholas was detained. He saw what appeared to be a green glow coming from the cracks in the old oak door. The wooden structure was nothing more than several four by fours slapped together and cut to fit, unequal in length, and held together by rusted metal.

The key cracked and popped as the Bishop turned the lock. The door creaked open.

"Good God, your face?" said a startled Bishop as he continued to stare, his mouth hanging open in confusion, his eyebrows scrunched together.

"What's wrong with my face?" Nicholas answered with a rasp whisper.

"It's glowing…like a candle!" the Bishop replied, scanning it in disbelief, softly taking Nicholas's arm and escorting him out of the room. He tried not to stare, but the green radiance stole his curiosity. He was mystified.

"Your confinement time is up, my friend. I hope you discovered the obedience necessary."

Nicholas quickly returned, "My obedience will always be to the Lord, Christ Jesus."

"Come eat, dear friend. The kitchen is open."

Smells of the evening's soup spilled from the kitchen and down the hallways. The fragrance was unusually welcomed by Nicholas's senses. He absorbed nothing but bread and water for the previous month and a half, and that, only once a day.

The monks were sitting around the table and already eating when Nicholas entered the dining hall. He felt the stares and could hear the gasps as they gazed at the luminescence on his face.

Nicholas took his usual place across from Jude. Jude nodded. Another monk came and placed a bowl of soup in front of the weary, hungry ex-prisoner, trying hard not to spill the soup as he observed the glow.

Nicholas dipped his spoon in the bowl and was about to take a sip when he noticed the vacant seat next to Jude. Concerned, Nicholas asked, "Where's Peter?"

Jude quietly explained, "He's very ill, my friend. They don't expect him to make it through the night."

"How long has he been ill?" Nicholas's heart pumped with terror for his closest friend and dear brother in the Lord.

"Almost as long as you've been gone."

Without hesitation, Nicholas dropped his spoon, jumped up from the table, and ran out of the room.

"Where are you going? You didn't even eat!" said Jude.

The young monk walked into Peter's cold, clammy room to find him lying on his back, one with his cot. Peter's face was almost as green as Nicholas's. His hair was matted and mangled, and his body glistened in sweat.

The smell of death lingered in the air, like a spirit waiting to take its victim.

Upon seeing Nicholas, Peter's excitement broke him into a series of coughs, followed by wheezing. Nicholas slowly knelt down beside Peter's bed, grasping Peter's hand with his right hand, and placing his left hand on Peter's forehead. Peter trembled. The beginnings of a smile played upon Peter's face.

"Lord, heal my brother Peter, whom you love. Show your mercy," Nicholas prayed fervently, but with a soft, soothing tone as he lifted Peter's hand and placed his face against it.

Bishop Bartholomew walked in. "Brother Nicholas, the Cardinal wants to see you after supper."

The chapel was a sacred room with dark oak beams interrupted by light flickering from hanging lanterns. Cardinal St. Michaels was kneeling at the altar when young Nicholas walked in behind him. Sensing his presence, the Cardinal turned around and jumped, startled by the green light lingering on Nicholas's face. He examined him for a moment, then turned away, noticeably unnerved, leaving his back to the young monk.

"You have tonight to pack your things. In the morning you'll be transferred to Myra. There they will talk with you about your probation."

"Probation?"

"It came to my attention that there was an indiscretion between you and a certain young lady." The Cardinal paused, then washed his hands in the Holy Water.

"Den mother Sarah?"

"An indiscretion?"

"You were kissing in the kitchen, were you not? God knows what else the two of you have been doing! She's already been released from her position." Judgment hung thick in the air as the Cardinal walked briskly past Nicholas and out of the chapel.

Nicholas took a moment to gather his thoughts and take in the presence of God. It had been a number of years since Nicholas's return to Myra. The thought excited him and troubled him at the same time. He was born in its small village, becoming a resident of its orphanage after a mere twelve years of his life. His parents were buried in Myra's catacombs nestled in the cliffs off the coast.

It was the sunniest day of the season, a perfect day for travel, although the low clouds promised blankets of snow by evening. Brother Nicholas and Bishop Bartholomew gathered their things and prepared the horse-driven sled for the day's journey. The monastery stood looming down on them, as if looking upon them with disapproval. Her shadow covered them like a dark curse. Nicholas took a cursory glance at it. A few monks were saying their farewells. Bishop Bartholomew wiggled the reins and the auburn steed started moving forward.

"Wait! Wait!" Peter yelled, running after them in his bedclothes. The Bishop stopped the horse. Peter tried to catch his breath.

"Peter, are you insane? You should be in bed!" the fatherly Bishop scolded.

"I had to say goodbye! Last night, after Nicholas prayed for me, the Lord healed me. I saw a bright light in my room. I felt something lift off of me. I thought I was dead, but then the fever left me. I feel fine now, I really do!"

Nicholas wrapped his arms around Peter's neck. His grip was tight.

"Goodbye, my dear friend. I will miss you," he murmured fiercely in Peter's ear.

"God bless you, Nicholas." Peter watched as the two robed men disappeared into the horizon.

Two days later.

The snow fell heavily as the strong winds hushed the sounds of anything in its path. The three boys were exhilarated to see such a February storm, but wondered how they'd make their planned escape to live with Brother Nicholas in Myra. The blizzard was so strong that it masked the sound of the hefty butcher's knocks from being heard, until his fourth and final time.

"Can we help you?" Bishop Bartholomew offered, as he and a few curious youth opened the back door near the kitchen.

The butcher was shivering. His clothes were stained in blood, and snow clung to him. He politely waited to be invited inside as the Cardinal's curiosity led him to the door with the others.

Seeing that the invitation wasn't open, the butcher caught his breath and spoke, "Is Brother Nicholas around?"

The entourage just looked at him. He was a little rough around the edges, as most butchers were. He didn't always know how to speak to others, and perhaps his beard and appearance were quite scruffy and intimidating. He thought he'd try another approach.

"I brought you some meats for the orphanage. I got caught in the storm…"

The Cardinal interrupted him, "Weren't you one of the men responsible for bringing goods to Brother Nicholas on the eve of the Festival of the Christ?"

The butcher's belly puffed out as he relaxed, smiled, and responded, "Yes, that's me…"

"Your meat was rancid. We threw it out. Do you really think you are doing the orphans a favor by giving them rotten meat?" claimed the cocky Cardinal.

The butcher's stance changed as he defended himself, denying the false accusation. "I gave you fresh meat, perfectly cut…"

"Sour," the Cardinal answered with his nose held high in the air.

"I gave you the best I had."

"Well, what does that say about you?" the Cardinal condemned. "We don't want your meat!"

The butcher was shifting on his feet, trying to keep his cool. If this was an ordinary man he was dealing with, the red caped figure would have been knocked out by now. But he couldn't justify hitting a man of God. He took a few deep breaths, studied the children's faces, and calmed himself down.

"Look, I have a cart full of meat. This blizzard's shut down the market for at least a week. It *will* go bad if someone doesn't take it," he pleaded, in a purposely calming tone.

"We have plenty of food. Good day, sir," the Cardinal ended the conversation, slamming the door in the butcher's face.

The Cardinal could hear the butcher's threats through the closed door.

Meanwhile, Jake, Darius, and Johansen found themselves escaping as the Cardinal and the butcher argued. The butcher's cart was full of raw meats from the day before. The carcasses were as big as the boys themselves, and covered with a thick burlap covering. The boys climbed in the cart, hiding under the covering, their clothes and hands stained from the bloody remains they were sitting against. They had planned their escape, and so far it appeared to be working perfectly.

By morning, the blizzard had stopped, and the kitchen crew of monks and children began making breakfast for the orphanage. One of the orphans opened the back door to let the cool air in as they usually did while they were cooking over the hot boiling pots. He shrieked at his discovery, which blocked the door from fully opening.

Brother Brian and the other children rushed to the back door and witnessed several large pieces of bloodied meat blocking the doorway from the outside. The carcasses were fresh.

"What is it?" one of the boys shouted, aghast.

Hearing the scream, Bishop Bartholomew and several of the children made their way into the kitchen to view the large mass of meat, covered in crimson snow.

One of the boys started crying, "Johansen, Darius, and Jake ran away last night and didn't come home!"

"And you knew about this and didn't tell us?" accused the Bishop. "How did they escape?"

Nathan, the scrawny leader of the bunch, whined out, "They were going to climb into the butcher's cart!"

By now several of the kids were crying.

Bishop Bartholomew looked at Nathan, then, slowly turned to look at the three large pieces of bloodied meat at the back door. He thought about the missing boys, then, looked back at Nathan, and back to the carcasses again before losing consciousness and passing out in the middle of the floor.

It had been a few days and the entire orphanage was mourning over the loss of the boys. Bishop Bartholomew received a telegram from Brother Nicholas that read:

My dearest Bishop,

I have learned of your sadness for Johansen, Darius, and Jake. I will find a way to bring them back to you. It may take a few days. Be in prayer.

Sincerely,
Brother Nicholas

The Bishop shared his letter with the Cardinal.

"Dear God, do you think he's going to use witchcraft to try to bring them back?" the Cardinal mocked, not realizing the three were safely in Myra.

A few days had passed and the three missing boys knocked on the door of the monastery. Jude opened the door, gawked at the boys, then, yelled for the Bishop.

Bishop Bartholomew hurried his way to the front door to observe the three young men standing there, still covered in bloody stains from head to toe. His knees gave way and the Bishop fainted again, slamming his head on the floor.

Chapter 5

Seventeen years later.

The view was epic and serene. For more than a decade, monk Nicholas found himself atop the cliffs in Myra, facing bluer-than-blue waters that shimmered in the sunlight. The breeze sang gently across the top of the hills, blades of deep green grass swaying to her melodies. It swept across Nicholas's face and he breathed it in. This was his escape. This was his alone time with God.

His previous Bishop took the young monk under his wing and trained him in a life of love and service. He encouraged young Nicholas to find God along the coastline. The two shared many mission trips together, but Myra was where Nicholas loved to be the most. The former Bishop knew of Nicholas's passion for the water, for boats, and for the smell of the salt sea air. He, too, knew what it was like to stand on the edge of the earth where the water met sand, and sense the presence of God.

He had encouraged Nicholas to talk to the sailors when they sailed into the harbor, looking for opportunities to share God's plan of salvation with them. Many of them came to know Nicholas personally, and appreciated his greetings. Some offered him gifts in exchange for a blessing. Foreigners felt welcomed by the young man in cloth who loved the sea, and enjoyed hearing stories of a God-man they'd never known. When sick ones arrived, Nicholas would pray for healing and God would display his power.

He even took a few small boating trips and learned to sail with some of the fishermen. They felt it was a good omen to bring a man of God on board, and he enjoyed the experiences. They equated a great day's catch to Nicholas's presence.

Many times he would return to the monastery smelling like fish. The other monks made fun of him at first, but they got used to the smell and appreciated the fish dinners.

"Bishop St. Joses…" Nicholas said out loud to himself, "a man of God." He thought about their many adventures together, and how he watched his mentor humbly allow God to produce several miracles through him. How odd that he died from the same disease of the girl that God healed through him. She was delivered from the irreversible plague just moments following his prayer. He contracted it shortly after and didn't survive. What a mystery. He was where he wanted to be, though.

He was, in fact, with Jesus. The beauty of Myra's beaches paled in comparison to a heavenly paradise.

The breeze became a little biting and Nicholas knew that winter would soon be upon him.

Peter sat on his cot at the Patara Monastery. His beard had thickened, and his eyes were softer. He fondled a feathered pen as he wrote.

My dearest friend, Nicholas,

I am writing to inform you that I have heard of all the wonderful things that our good Lord Christ Jesus is doing through you. I have heard how angels follow you and healing flows from your touch. I know that you have continued with your tradition of blessing Myra's orphans during the Festival of the Christ, and I am pleased at the announcement of your benediction, receiving the title of BISHOP for your obedience and work in the Lord. I am sending you this letter to inform you of my intent to be present for your benediction and am requesting a transfer to serve you permanently at the Myra Monastery.

Sincerely in Christ,
Peter

The Myra Monastery was a bit smaller and older than Patara. It was also more welcoming. Windows and open doorways lined every room, wall and walkway, filling each space with unlimited measures of natural light. Brother Nicholas closed the letter from Peter and slowly looked up to Heaven. His heart gazed at the thought of having his best friend serve with him again. Nicholas had also grown a small beard. He laughed at the thought of comparing it to Peter's.

His smile quickly fell as his memories taunted him. The monastery at Patara was more like a dark, dismal dungeon to him. It was God's testing time, God's wilderness for a young Nicholas. His grin slowly returned as he thought about the children, and of course, the beautiful morning of the Festival of the Christ. His heart pounded in exhilaration as he pictured the smiles on the children's faces as they found their gifts. He thought about how they were all adults now, with kids of their own, he assumed. Perhaps Patara wasn't that bad, after all.

Myra's chapel was at full capacity. More than forty monks dressed in brown robes sang in unison as they entered the room and took their place along the rear wall. The music was heavenly. An older, wiser Nicholas stood at the front of the room, dressed in a crème under-robe. He took a moment to make eye contact and smile at each monk as they sang. Many returned the gesture, proud of their comrade in the Lord. Bishop St. Claire stood beside him wearing crimson and gold with a gold crown and holding a wooden staff. The Archbishop made his way into the room and the monks hushed. He was wearing a white robe and a tall white crown. He picked up a long, lit white candle filled with wet candle wax and walked over to Nicholas.

"The hand of the Lord is upon you. Today you will exchange your robe of humility and denial for a robe of service. The robe you wear represents the blood of Christ. May you always remember His sacrifice."

The Archbishop then poured the melted wax over Nicholas's right shoulder, followed by the left. It burned his skin a little.

"May these tassels always remind you that you are in service to the Lord," finished the Archbishop.

Bishop St. Claire took the red robe and placed it on Nicholas. He then handed him a stripped down wooden staff that stood about five feet tall.

The Archbishop proceeded, "May this staff remind you that you are a shepherd of the Lord in Myra, that you are to gently guide these people in the ways of the Lord, just as the Lord gently guides you."

Nicholas bowed his head as Bishop St. Claire placed a tall, white crown upon it.

"May this be a remembrance that you wear a helmet of salvation. Wear it proudly as you speak to the people from the chancel. May God bless you and be with you, Nicholas, Bishop of Myra."

The monks chanted another song as the Archbishop made his way out. Nicholas breathed in the excitement. With humility and honor the new Bishop lifted his eyes to the Lord and then slowly bowed his head. He had dreams for the town of Myra, and as their Bishop, he hoped to serve the people and his community with a Christ-like heart, bringing those dreams into fruition.

Bishop St. Claire was sifting through the scrolls scattered on the desk of the Bishop's office. Nicholas made his way into the room.

"Still no transfer from Patara?"

The Bishop sighed at Nicholas. "I'm sorry, friend, all of our communication has been cut off for fear of the Roman soldiers. Peter may have been intercepted on his journey."

Bishop St. Claire walked over to Nicholas and kindly touched his shoulder. As Nicholas turned around, they met eye to eye.

"Have a safe journey, Nicholas. Rome would love to capture a man of God, such as you."

"You too have a safe journey back to your monastery. Thank you for filling in," Nicholas murmured, appreciating the kindness.

"Bishop St. Joses was a dear friend of mine. He will be greatly missed. I'm sure he's watching down on us from Heaven, and I know he's proud of you. I know you'll do a great job taking care of Myra."

"I'll do my God-given best," answered a humbled Nicholas.

Bishop St. Claire turned around and continued to fumble through the scrolls, deciding which ones to take and which ones to leave. "You are such a servant to the people. But risking your life for lower taxes and better food isn't worth it. We take care of the people here. Their taxes are raised; so we feed them, give them extra clothes. We pray for them. We don't meet the devil eye-to-eye and argue with him. You're responsible for this monastery now, and the people who need you here."

"That's why I *must* go. Pray that the good Lord is with me, protecting me from the enemies' claws," Nicholas said earnestly.

The newly-ordained Bishop Nicholas, along with his help—monks David, Phillip, and Marcus—made their way to a small town on their journey towards Byzantium, also named the new Rome. The trio of monks was excited about their first mission trip, even if it was a life threatening one. The Bishop picked these men based upon their abilities, or lack of, and hoped to get to know and mentor each of them on their passage.

Nicholas saw David as the brains of the operation. He placed the map in his hands and trusted him for direction and timing, aligning their journey in the way of safety, yet still hitting enough small towns to be well fed without drawing too much attention to men of the cloth.

Phillip was a curly-haired, scrawny man who was great with a horse, meals, and setting camp. He was athletic and often restless inside the monastery. Nicholas could sense it and thought he'd be great for the operation.

Contrary to the others, Marcus was a sensitive, caring monk without many talents, who loved children, loved God, and loved his new Bishop. Love was his skill. Nicholas had a tender spot in his heart for Marcus, and made him his apprentice.

David and Phillip set the pace while Bishop Nicholas rode on the back of the white stallion, Marcus holding the reins.

The four men of God traveled for quite some time before they reached their first destination: a small, unknown town on the winding road northwest of Myra. It was a great place for rest and recovery.

A crippled beggar sat at the gates of the town entrance. He was clothed in blemished rags and exposed his rotted teeth as he offered a crooked, delirious smile. Sweaty and dirty, with bloodshot eyes and matted, greasy hair, his lack of grooming provoked little sympathy from passerby. His left leg was deformed and protruding from the clothes that covered it. He pleaded with Nicholas as other townsfolk noticed the travelers arriving. They were making their way over to meet Bishop Nicholas when he stepped down from the horse and put some money in the beggar's cup. He also touched the man's head and said a silent prayer for him.

A voice yelled in the distance, "Saint Nicholas!"

A woman jabbered to another, "Is that him?"

The crowd pressed in. A young boy brought water for the horse as people strove to touch the Bishop. They were all too excited about meeting "God's anointed one," or as some called him, "The Healer," that they didn't even notice that the crippled beggar's leg was completely healed, and that he walked away, praising God through Main Street.

"My master said that you might stay with us. We have plenty of room for you and your men," said a young fellow with dark olive skin and curly brown hair.

The house was ornate with beautiful woodcarvings and candle designs. Nicholas and the housemaster sat at a uniquely carved table made of mahogany, each leg and corner formed with impeccable detail. The boy servant placed drinks on the table in front of them.

"...The entire table was carved out of one piece of wood," the housemaster bragged.

"Amazing... Did you do all these wood carvings yourself?" asked an impressed Nicholas, gently caressing the table with his hand and inspecting the wood articles across the room.

The housemaster quickly finished his sip and placed his cup down. "Oh, no! I could only dream of doing such work."

Even the very cup that Nicholas held was carved out of wood and displayed an etched scene of a winter village with impeccable detail.

"Incredible, isn't it?"

Nicholas tilted his head to the side and continued his inspection while twisting the cup around with his fingers. "Now how on earth can someone carve something so small?"

"Little hands."

Nicholas scrunched his forehead. "Children?"

Both men laughed. The housemaster declined to respond.

Nicholas, Marcus, and the housemaster talked fourth century art for quite some time before hitting a more serious note.

The housemaster leaned forward to warn the Bishop, "...Diocletian has written a decree to imprison anyone who professes Christ. Why would you endanger yourself by going to Byzantium? Please, I beg you not to go."

"I sent two of my most noble monks ahead of me. If there is danger ahead, they will let us know."

"We need to pray that they aren't captured. It could bring danger to all of us."

A cold chill filled the new morning air, evident by the puffs of vapor escaping from the horse's nostrils. Marcus prepared their horse for the day's journey as Nicholas said his final farewell.

"Bishop! Bishop!" exclaimed a young monk named Cornelius, as he ran into the stable, out of breath. "I'm glad I caught you before you left," the words spewed from his lips, out of rhythm.

"Catch your breath, young monk," Nicholas responded. His eyes were doubtful.

"It's the Cardinal!"

"Is he okay? Is he hurt? What's wrong?" Nicholas put his hand on Cornelius's back, as the young monk was still bent over trying to breathe.

"The Cardinal doesn't want you to go to Byzantium! Diocletian is expecting you. They plan on arresting you when you get there."

Marcus carefully interrupted, "They know we're coming? That means that David and Phillip were probably arrested!"

Cornelius continued, "The Cardinal said to make your way home a different path. It's too risky to return the way you came."

"Dear brother, you may lead the way."

"If I may decline, Bishop. I am a runner and promised the Cardinal that I would return to deliver a message of your safety."

"For your journey," the housemaster offered as he placed a purple velvet bag of coins in Nicholas's hand. "It's modern Roman currency. You may need it."

Marcus thanked the man for his hospitality and took the horse's reins.

"So you know a better way?" Bishop Nicholas prodded the housemaster.

"Through the forest, up in the mountains to the north," he said as he pointed with his finger, and followed with his eyes. "There is a small, less traveled path that's only known by the locals. You'll be safe from soldiers, but you need to be careful about bandits. Try to make it through the thick of it before sundown. You'll know when you are through it. Oh, and your horse will never make it. You can leave him here. I will have him returned to the monastery. Blessings to you, Saint Nicholas."

"I'm not a saint."

"With all due respect," interjected the housemaster, "a true saint isn't just a title given by your superior in the church. A saint is measured by his actions."

"Then, my friend, you are a saint too. Thank you for your kindness."

Chapter 6

The old clay road was brittle with stone chips. Vacant buildings barely stood to the left and right, with an abandoned orchard after that on the right side. A small forest began on the left. Bishop Nicholas and his novice made their way down the less traveled road to avoid attention and possible arrest. A freckly-faced, tough-looking thirteen-year-old boy with wild, bushy red hair made a fast pass towards Nicholas, and tried to grab a satchel hanging off of his belt. The Bishop quickly grasped the boy's arm and held on tightly.

"Poor technique! What's your name?" Nicholas questioned the boy, undaunted by the attempt at thievery.

The boy tried to force himself free from Nicholas's grip. The Bishop finally let go, freeing his hands to open the possession desired: his satchel of food.

"If it's food you want, I have plenty to share. Don't be afraid, boy."

The young runaway street boy approached Nicholas timidly and held out his hand to receive something.

Nicholas placed a carrot in his palm and said, "What's your name, boy?" in a calming manner.

"My name's S… S… Stu," the young teen stuttered.

As Stu took a bite of the crisp carrot, two other homeless street teens ran out from the woods and abandoned buildings where they were hiding and begged Nicholas for food too. He handed the three of them the rest of the food in his satchel. They devoured it all in seconds.

"I can help you get more."

The boys accompanied the Bishop and the monk for a good part of the day's journey. Once they felt comfortable enough, they told the men of their past trials and adventures. They were all orphans, not because they were abandoned, but because they chose to be, according to Stu. Being a street kid meant being tough and unconnected to any adult, and the boys shared stories that supported this theory.

Nicholas just listened and waited for God to give him an opportunity to share with the young teens. They trusted him, and he built that trust by being a listening ear. They didn't care if he was a man of the cloth or not. He fed their hunger pangs. He promised even more. And unlike their parents, he was already showing interest in their tales of wild escapades, regardless of how fictionalized they became.

According to Stu, there were more than a dozen runaway teens living together in the abandoned buildings near the broken road where they met, but that many of them had been arrested or taken captive by the Roman soldiers. Nicholas sniggered at their stories of fighting off the soldiers with slingshots and escaping from them through the forest. Of course, the soldiers were more than seven, no eight, maybe ten feet tall, and marched in groups of a hundred says their saga. And yet, the three boys now freely walking the streets with the man in red all managed to escape the score of dreaded warriors.

Stu was in mid-sentence when Nicholas held up his hand, hushed the brigade, and surveyed their surroundings. He watched the path as it curved down the gently rolling hills, fading beyond the prairie swells, disappearing and then reappearing near the horizon. Patches of brown and green painted the landscape. Just past the curve, Nicholas spotted what appeared to be some kind of crop, and quickly redirected the boys to it.

Bishop Nicholas, Marcus, and the street boys stood in the middle of the cornfields. The sun offered one more hour of light. They were all breaking off heads of the corn and placing them into Nicholas's bag. The stalks looked sickly with wilted, fading green, yellow and brown leaves, and the band was sifting through, searching for the healthier ones.

Marcus addressed Nicholas, "Um, isn't this stealing?"

"No." He smiled.

"No?"

By the time they reached the oversized, ancient house that sat between the cornfields and sheep pens, the sun had almost faded behind the earth. It was difficult to see, but Nicholas could tell that the home had been standing for almost a century. It was a wealthy man's home, but there was nothing fancy about it except its size— a key sign that Rome didn't own it. It was a wonder that the Roman government hadn't confiscated it. There was plenty of land to farm, ranch, and produce. It would be an asset to the Roman Empire. Perhaps it was too well hidden and far enough out of the way that the Romans didn't see a need for it, or even notice it.

Nicholas knocked on the weathered wooden door of the wealthy man's home. A tall, distinguished man, pushing his seventies, opened the door slightly, trying to depict the politeness of a gentleman, and yet quite fearful and curious at the same time. He was startled by the sight of Nicholas and his entourage, but relaxed after recognizing the Bishop's robe as a symbol of holiness and peace. He himself was not a religious man, but he welcomed anyone who came in peace. The old man hadn't had any visitors since the Roman invasion began. He was still hesitant, inquisitive as to why the men of the cloth and dirty teenage boys were there, in the middle of nowhere.

"Sir, we picked some corn from your fields for you," offered Nicholas, as he showed the man the bag filled with kernels.

The man glanced down and quickly surveyed the sack. "I have servants to do that. Besides, can't you see that my corn isn't exactly ripe this year?" His voice cracked, shifting like a boy in puberty, aged but nervous.

"There's a cold front coming. Your crops probably wouldn't survive that anyway." Nicholas leaned in and spoke softly, "These boys are hungry." He slipped the man a gold coin outside of the boys' vision.

"I'll see what I can do for you," the man answered, and then turned around as if he needed approval from someone else in the next room.

Nicholas caught his attention again. "I have one more favor to ask of you before we dine tonight." He then pulled out another gold coin and handed it to the man, placing it in his wrinkled, dry, spotted hand. The man squeezed the coin tightly, as if not to drop it.

Marcus and the boys sat around a square wooden table filled with delicacies. There was turkey, quail, cranberries, greens, and three different kinds of breads, plenty of dipping oils and spices, and corn, to name a few. Long-lasting smiles of ecstasy graced each one of their faces.

Nicholas walked in the room and caught everyone's attention. "Well, let's bless the food!" he said, seemingly oblivious as everyone stared.

The boys started laughing. Marcus eyed the Bishop up and down, confused by the costume. Even Nicholas himself felt a little odd wearing the rich man's clothes, but it provided a perfect disguise.

After his prayer, the boys stuffed their faces as if they'd never eaten before.

"You better slow down or you'll get a stomachache," fathered Nicholas.

"Aren't you eating anything?" asked one of the boys, noticing Nicholas's plate was empty.

"He only eats twice a week," replied Marcus, in between bites. "I know. He appears crazy."

"More for me!" answered Stu, happily biting into a thick slice of meat.

Nicholas interrupted as if his thoughts were elsewhere. "We're going to Byzantium." Everyone stopped eating and gawked at him. Marcus's eyes widened as he exhaled a breath of exhaustion and frustration. This could be a death trap, he thought to himself.

The boys began their journey down the steps of the rich man's home as Marcus and the newly-disguised wealthy man Nicholas, turned around to say goodbye.

"Again, thank you." The Bishop firmly shook the man's hand. "Do you want a blessing on your crops?"

"There's been an awful drought this year...," the man said, making excuses.

Nicholas interrupted and asked again, "Do you want a blessing on your crops?"

The man stood silent, his lack of faith evident by the look on his face.

"Give it away," Nicholas offered.

"Give it away?"

"Yes. Give it away. You know what I mean."

The lonely old man had plenty to share with a starving region. But the business man he was trained to be never gave him permission to give anything away. Just the thought of it caused his heart to race. He was a victim to his thoughts and practices, and he was about to lose it all. He had a choice.

Bishop Nicholas and Marcus made their way down the steps and past the first few rows of cornfields. As Nicholas walked by them, slowly and steadily the stalks in the field miraculously turned dark green and gained stature, standing up tall and healthy. The boys gasped in wonder at the affair.

After a few cold nights and a weary afternoon's walk, Nicholas and his crew found themselves at the gate of Byzantium. This new city was designed as a temporary headquarters for Rome while the Roman soldiers conquered new lands to the east. It wasn't fully developed because the plans were to abandon the area once their quest was complete. However, Rome's signature was etched in every detail of the place.

The boys stared in amazement at the architecture. There were a sea of stone and clay buildings surrounding them, and marketers shouting their sales with authority.

"Marcus, get lost. I'll meet you here in an hour," ordered a determined Nicholas, handing Marcus his crimson bag of clothes and goodies. Nicholas made his way through the crowd unnoticed in his costume. Stu and his friends closely followed.

They walked past high concrete archways, houses made of stone and marble, bridges unimaginable, and uniquely displayed stone carved statues. They gazed at the market: scrumptious red apples, winter green olives and cucumbers, oils and spices, fancy shawls, scarves, and shoes in a variety of colors, hens and eggs by the hundreds, lambs wool, homemade soup, etc. Any want or desire could be met here—for a price.

Young, beautiful women dressed in silky, colorful linens aligned outside one of the fancy, marble buildings to the right. They called to the boys, waving and flirting. Nicholas redirected the young men's eyes to the structure ahead. They reached a grand arena at least ten stories high, with masks cut into stone along the outside wall. They could see the beautiful arches across the top floor from the backside of the dome.

"Whoa! I wonder if this place ever fills up?" said one of the teens.

"Probably. This city is the new heart of the world," answered Nicholas.

Stu questioned, "What do they do in there?"

"Let's not find out," Nicholas quickly reacted, walking briskly past it, while still admiring its architecture. He had heard rumors about such a structure in Rome and how Christians were often put on display in the previous decades. Seen as game for the Roman citizens, the Christian prisoners were bet on how long they would survive against a wild animal. Although he hadn't heard of that happening in Byzantium, he was a historian, and as all historians know, history repeats itself.

They arrived at the door of the Emperor's headquarters, heavily guarded by two soldiers holding spears and sheathed swords hanging from their belts. The headquarters looked more like a modern day, three-story home, with three columns at its entrance and royal flags hanging from the front. Sketches of Rome's warriors were carved into its walls.

"And what business do you have with the Emperor?"

Nicholas pulled out a gold coin. "It's a matter of finances and welfare." He tossed the coin and the guard caught it. "I've come to make a plea for the people."

The Roman guard made his way behind the doorway for a minute, and quickly returned.

"Follow me."

The Emperor of Byzantium, Diocletian, slouched sideways against a large gold chair covered in burgundy velvet. He flipped the coin Nicholas gave the guard between his fingers.

"Do I know you?" the Emperor asked Nicholas.

"No," Nicholas responded nervously.

"I can see by your clothes and your generosity that you are a man of stature. And what have you come for?"

Nicholas pushed out his chest, took a deep breath, and stared sternly at Diocletian's eyes. "I have come in response to the outcry of the people."

Diocletian broke the eye contact by throwing his head back and laughing. "And what outcry is that?" He massaged the gold coin against the velvet chair.

"Emperor, the people of commons are starving. There is little food, and the taxes are too much to bear."

"And what region are you from?" Diocletian asked, confused, almost amused that someone would complain about such a great, thriving city.

"East…"

"Ah. I see." Diocletian thought little of the cities that stretched to the coastline. He saw them as useless except for taxing the few imports and exports that came by sea.

"There is a black market because marketers can't afford to sell with Rome's consent anymore."

Diocletian snidely commented, "And you're worried how this hurts your business? It's always about money."

"No. I'm here for the people." Nicholas hesitated. "I'm worried for the families who are starving, living in the streets because Rome took even the little that they did have."

The Emperor paused as if he was taking it in, then, belittled Nicholas's plea, as if he didn't even hear him.

"Problem solved! Show me the black marketers and we'll get rid of them!"

The disguised Bishop shook his head in disbelief. "Emperor, that's not the answer."

"How does it affect *you*?" Diocletian pressed, targeting Nicholas's motives.

Another pause.

"Who are the young boys you brought with you?" the Emperor sniffed, changing position in his chair.

"These boys are homeless, a result of your new taxation. I found them on the way here. They're starvers."

Diocletian stood up, walked over to the boys and inspected them as if they were a foreign species.

"Where are your parents, boy?"

"I don't know," spoke a timid voice.

"You don't know?" he questioned Stu, condescendingly. Diocletian paused, waiting for an answer, and realized one wasn't coming. He walked over to Nicholas and stood in front of him, hoping to intimidate him.

"And what do you suppose we do with these children?"

Nicholas coughed. "Someone needs to take care of them. Make sure they're fed, clothed, and learn an honest trade."

"And what do you expect me to do about that?"

"Not ignore that there is a need. Unless something is done, you will see more and more children living among the streets, and your crime will increase. I beg of you, Emperor, in view of God's mercy, help the people. Lower the taxes and provide food. Help these children."

"Leave the boys with me. I'll see what I can do. My guards will help you find your way out." He watched for Nicholas's response, hoping to find a way to trap him in a lie. If the boys were just pretending to be homeless, then Nicholas would refuse to leave them behind, he assumed.

Nicholas nodded to the boys and left the room as two guards followed. The Emperor took his seat.

The afternoon crowd had thickened among the dusty city streets. Nicholas approached the entrance to Byzantium once again as Marcus watched from a distance. Two beggars sat at the gate, hoping for a handout from any new visitors that walked by.

"Please," said the closest beggar, holding up his cup towards the nicely dressed Nicholas. His face was partially deformed with leprosy.

Nicholas touched the man on the head and said, "In the name of Jesus Christ, be healed."

With a confused look on his face, the leper held his cup up just a moment longer before lowering it, realizing that he wasn't going to receive any coins. Nicholas began to undress and laid his coat over the cups of the two men. Hidden in the throng of people, Marcus made his way to Nicholas and opened his bag to pull out the Bishop's robe.

"Holy Jesus!" exclaimed the second street beggar, as he stared at the face of his leprous friend.

"What?" replied the leper, then, touched his own face as it supernaturally healed beneath his fingertips.

Chapter 7

The hazy orange sun was setting behind the hills as Nicholas and Marcus walked the much-traveled path. They heard the sound of hurried pitter-patter coming at them. Nicholas turned around quickly enough to see the young boy scream and try to tackle him. His arms were flailing, his head pressed hard against Nicholas's chest, wiry orange hair flying everywhere.

Nicholas just held the young lad.

"You left me there!" The youngster cried out as his arms stopped swinging and wrapped themselves around Nicholas. The child began sobbing in the Bishop's arms.

Nicholas didn't know what to say. He knew that nothing would make sense to a teenage boy fearing abandonment for a second time. First his parents, and now a trusted man of the cloth. A young boy doesn't understand that any rebellion from the Emperor meant death. Nicholas had no choice.

"They're coming! They're coming after you! They know who you are!" Stu shouted. His clothes were torn and blood graced his brow and chin from a recent brawl.

"Did you fight the guards?" Nicholas asked, amused.

Nicholas leaned against the tall stone statue standing on the side of the road, pushing with all his might. Artemis, one of the many gods of the local people stood a proud but silent fifteen feet tall or more, encircled by a stone temple.

"Don't just stand there! Help me!" Nicholas shouted, as he tried to push the statue over.

"I don't know about this. If we get caught for this, we'll be stoned for sure," Marcus said as he watched Nicholas. "You're pushing over their god."

"Yeah, but she's not *the* God. She's a false god. And she has no place in this city!"

Stu and Marcus looked at each other cautiously before helping push Artemis over. One by one they broke the stones in the temple until none were standing. Nicholas took a stone and pounded the head of Artemis until it was almost unrecognizable.

The temperature dropped as the crimson sky set in, leaving a cold chill in the air, a scent of evil ever so present. Diocletian and several of his soldiers made their way to the entrance of Byzantium's city gate while riding horses adorned for battle. Something caught the Emperor's eye and he halted his painted horse so quickly that it almost threw him off the back of it.

"Wait a minute. Don't I know you?" he asked the man playing cards at the city gate. The gambler's smooth, soft face glowed by the fire. He was wearing a wealthy man's coat—the very coat Nicholas left at the entrance of the city.

The Emperor paused, staring at the card player. "Good God, you're that leper that always hangs out here!

What happened to your face?" he barked with bewilderment.

Before the healed beggar had a chance to speak, his friend spoke up excitedly, "It was St. Nicholas! He was here!"

The Emperor demanded, "Did he say where he was going?"

The two beggars looked sideways at each other. "Somewhere very cold: the North Pole?" the healed beggar shared in a sarcastic, almost comical tone.

Diocletian kicked his heels and his horse sprung to action, but not before he had the opportunity to kick over the tall fire that kept the gamblers warm.

The two men of God and their tag-a-long teen warily approached the small town once again, hoping to find refuge in the home of the kind housemaster that took them in weeks before. However, they did not receive the same greeting as their first visit from the townsfolk. In fact, they received no greeting at all. The streets were desolate without sight or sound. Doors of shops and homes would close as the three visitors walked by. It was a ghost town. Only, people actually lived there. They were seized by fear so greatly that not even the sick were willing to call out to the great Saint Nicholas for healing.

Nicholas knocked three times on the door of the housemaster's home. No one answered. He waited a few more minutes and knocked again. The housemaster opened the door quickly and pulled the travelers inside.

"What are you doing here? You must leave immediately," he said to the Bishop, in a soft, forced whisper. "They're looking for you. There's a price on your head. They've been snooping around town."

Before the housemaster could finish his sentence, another knock protruded through the door with great force. Nicholas, Marcus, and Stu quickly scampered through the house in search of hiding places while the housemaster's servant slowly opened the door. Four Roman soldiers forced their way in and began immediately rummaging through all of the rooms in search of the man of God. The housemaster followed them, watching in terror, praying that his dear friends would not be discovered.

One of the soldiers found the back door cracked open and followed footprints to a small guesthouse. The soldier forced the door open to the guesthouse to find Marcus tying a white rope belt around a ridiculously short servant outfit he was wearing.

"Who are you?" the soldier demanded.

"Uh, he's one of my house servants," the housemaster interjected.

The soldier snickered. "Don't you think your outfit's a little small?"

"I feed my servants well," the housemaster answered for him.

Marcus grinned, proud of himself for following in the footsteps of his mentor and Bishop, and for actually getting away with it!

The soldier pushed Marcus out of the way and continued his search in the small, single room guesthouse, spearing anything that looked like a place where a person could hide. He was concentrating so much on finding a physical being, he didn't notice his shoe catching in the sleeve of Marcus's brown robe laying on the ground. After the soldier untangled himself, he and one of his companions followed the frantic neighing of a horse in the barn.

Marcus wiped his brow in a sigh of relief and exhaled deeply.

The white stallion was calling attention to himself and anything else moving in the barn. The soldiers went through haystacks, thrusting their spears into every pile, looking in the troughs, behind stables, and everywhere they could think of. One of the soldiers stabbed something pretty solid as he pricked a haystack, but was distracted by the series of coughs coming from the housemaster's servant.

Meanwhile, two of the soldiers continued their dismantling of the main house, completely tearing apart the interior. The unique furniture was thrashed, beds were ripped apart, rooms were destroyed, and clothes, bins, baskets and basins were shredded into pieces. Almost nothing survived. Even the wood in the fireplace was pulled out and thrown about.

The soldiers quickly left and the housemaster, Marcus, and the servant, made their way back to the main house to survey the damage and to find the missing Bishop and the boy. The servant watched the soldiers leave through the window and nodded to the housemaster when they were far enough away.

"Bishop? If you are in here, they are gone," he called out in a quiet voice, the sound echoing in the room and through the halls.

They heard a rustling sound coming from the fireplace. The sound made its way down the chimney, and echoed in its shallow walls. They watched the mouth of the fireplace, expecting an animal to come crawling through.

They spotted two feet poking through the opening where the wood once stood, wiggling desperately to shake the figure free from the small, confined space. Recognizing the Bishop, the housemaster quickly helped pull him out.

"Ho! Ho! Ho!" the Bishop laughed and whimpered at the same time as they tugged on him, his hands and face black with soot. There were some minor cuts on his body, but considering the alternative to being arrested by Roman soldiers, he was feeling pretty good.

"Nice," the house master commented on the genius of Nicholas's hiding spot.

Nicholas asked, "Where's Stu?"

"We don't know. We can't find him," answered Marcus, who was still wearing the tiny servant outfit. The Bishop eyed him up and down a few times before laughing softly and shaking his head, proud of his apprentice.

The servant boy led them to the barn where the horse was still uneasy and they heard a whimpering sound coming from a stash of hay.

"Stu?" Nicholas called out.

Seeing strands of orange hair in the midst of a haystack, the housemaster dragged the boy out from under the hay and exposed his arm, bloodied from a Roman spear. He was crying but trying to hold it in, displaying the bravery of a thirteen year old young man.

The travelers quickly cleaned up and returned to their normal attire, while the servant cleaned out Stu's small wound. The spear barely nicked the young lad, but the arc was long, producing a wide bloodied cut. Luckily, the wound was bandaged easily and Stu was offered more clothing. The Housemaster loaded all three of them in the back of the hay wagon, forced them to lie down, and covered them with a leather blanket and some hay. After attaching the horse, he and the servant quickly took the men through town and up the path towards the forest and mountains.

They passed a few other travelers, but were suspicious to no one.

The moon shifted into focus as the sun began her descent. The elevation lifted and the trekkers found themselves in the thick of the forest at the base of the mountains east of Byzantium, but north of Myra. They had said their goodbyes a good hour's walk back, and the trio was exhausted.

"We should make camp here," suggested the Bishop.

Marcus looked around at the sun diminishing behind the trees. "You heard what the man said. Shouldn't we try to make it through the thick of it first?"

"We need to reserve our strength for tomorrow's journey. Besides, if we wait much longer, we may not be able to see well enough to make camp," said Nicholas, as he took the load off his shoulder. Something moved and startled Marcus and Stu.

"Did you guys hear that?"

"I'm sure it was nothing, Marcus. Besides, God is with us," answered Nicholas.

"I don't want to be something's dinner. Can we go just a little bit further?" clamored Stu.

Clickity clack! Ker-plop! Ker-plop!

Marcus pointed out a furry animal making its way quickly up the mountain rocks, silhouetted by the glowing sun divided by tree limbs. The elk-looking creature almost appeared like it was flying as it skipped up the rocks at high speeds and out of sight.

"Man, did you see that?" Stu said with childlike wonder and awe.

"What was it?" questioned Marcus.

The sky was congested with dark clouds. The only light visible was the faint flickers of the flames that died earlier in the night. Nicholas, Marcus, and Stu were lying side by side, their faces illuminated by the burning embers and distant moon.

"ZzzzzZZZzzzzz…" Nicholas wheezed himself into a deep sleep as Marcus responded with his own sleep language…

"Kashooo… Kashoooo…"

The nighttime wind tickled the leaves into laughter, producing a rustling sound that suffocated the thumps of little feet surrounding the two men and the boy.

Nicholas felt a presence over him. Startled by two small, round faces, the Bishop gasped, waking up his friends.

The grown men of the mountain forest stood approximately four feet tall at most. Waking up to see small people the size of primary children with beards and muscles is a little shocking at first. Marcus thought he was dreaming, or perhaps having a nightmare. Stu awoke, creating a high-pitched scream that rivaled any little girl in distress.

"Saint Nicholas, is that you?" the first little man's voice spoke like a record being played in a fast speed.

"We heard you were coming this way," the other little man interrupted.

Nicholas rubbed his eyes in disbelief, as if he were having a vision.

"Can you help us, Bishop? We're told you can heal our sister," pleaded Andy, the first dwarfed man.

"God does the healing. What's wrong with her?" slurred Nicholas, still trying to wake up from his slumber.

Impatiently, the dwarf explained, "She's very ill. She might die. But if you come and pray for her, we know she'll live. If you come and help us, we'll give you a place to sleep, some food to eat, and escort you through the forest safely."

"Safely?" Marcus questioned, wondering if they were even safe now.

The little men looked optimistically at Nicholas, shifting back and forth on their feet.

Nicholas asked, "How far is it?"

Harry, Andy's younger and shorter brother, spoke with a smile. "Not far, but you'll have to be blindfolded—all of you."

"Why do I get the feeling you've done this before?" Marcus said nervously.

"Uh huh!" Harry grinned and nodded.

Doubting their safety, Marcus questioned their trustworthiness.

Nicholas interrupted, "Marcus, have faith, brother. If they wanted to hurt us, they could have by now."

The journey was long and cold. Unaccustomed to the altitude, the three visitors continued popping their ears as they traveled through the mountainous woods. Blindfolded, they could feel the slush of snow beginning under their feet as they reached the higher altitudes.

"We must be getting pretty high up the mountain?" questioned Nicholas.

A non-response by the dwarfs didn't ease Marcus's fears.

"Can we rest? I can't breathe!" Stu expressed to the group, stopping to take big gulps of the thin mountain air.

"We can keep going. We're almost there," answered Harry, taking Stu by the arm, who felt much like a prisoner by now.

The blindfolds dropped, revealing an intricate community of finely carved, one-of-a-kind houses made of wood, marble and precious stone. The full moon rested on the mountain's crest, highlighting the magnificent detail of each wooden ornament. High triangular peaks graced the roofs to keep the snow from accumulating on top of the houses. Nicholas, Marcus, and Stu were at a loss for words.

The houses were all in a circle, facing one another. There were two and three story houses that looked as if they came out of a fairy tale, even if it was a fairy tale from the 4th Century. No human had ever witnessed such design. No known architect had ever dreamed of creating something so uniquely beautiful. There seemed to have been some Chinese architectural influences, but with a style all its own.

At first, it appeared as if there were only four or five houses. However, as Nicholas and his road crew took a deeper look, they could see all the white houses nestled in the woods, barely visible through the snowy tree limbs and white frosted ground.

Nicholas inhaled, speaking under his breath. "Magnificent."

"Come. Sharon's waiting." Harry guided them, taking Nicholas by the coat and leading him to the two story wooden and stone home.

"Um, I'm not blindfolded anymore. I could just follow you," Nicholas said in soft sarcasm.

Harry let go of his coat. "Oh, yeah. Sorry." He chuckled, grinning impishly.

As they walked, the heroic trio could see shadows of other dwarfs moving in the light, hoping to get a glimpse of the great Nicholas, healer of the sick.

"Are all of you..." Marcus tried to find a way to say it so that it didn't sound rude.

"Dwarfed like me?" Andy spoke up, almost expecting Marcus's comment.

Harry jumped in to break the awkwardness. "We're all like this. Little is beautiful," he said with a grin, causing all of them to laugh.

As they entered the house, Nicholas expected to see a dwarfed woman lying in bed, her tiny pointed shoes at the bedside, and miniature clothes hanging from her closet. None of the trio expected to see what they did see.

Andy's sister Sharon was lying on her back. Her eyes were shut and her face was pale. Her long, golden, auburn hair glistened from sweat and covered her shoulders. At first she appeared dead until she broke out in uncontrollable coughs.

Bishop Nicholas knelt slowly beside her. His eyes studied her face as if he found something he'd been looking for. He softly rubbed her forehead with the back of his hand and then caressed her cheek with his palm. She gained consciousness and locked eyes with Nicholas.

For a moment, it was as if no one else was in the room. There was an electric connection made—a chemistry that no mere scientist or sociologist could explain. Nicholas felt it. His heart pounded uncontrollably. The outside temperature had dropped from cold to freezing, but he was warm—too warm for a Bishop called to celibacy.

Sharon lost consciousness again, and Nicholas was reminded of why he was there. He placed his hand on her forehead and began to pray.

Andy quickly covered Sharon's foot that poked out from under the covers. Although she was short by normal standards, her five foot, two-and-a-half inch frame was a little long for the dwarf beds and covers.

Swirls of the sun's colors reflected on the forest's white carpet. Marcus and Nicholas sat on the floor of Andy's cottage house, staring at the scenery through the doorway. Unlike homes in their region, the floors were primarily made of wood boards, which weren't so harsh on little dwarf feet during the winter. The strong smell of bacon and eggs came from the kitchen. Andy handed Nicholas a plate.

"I'm sorry, I must decline," said Nicholas.

"You afraid of my cookin'?" asked Andy, smiling sweetly.

Marcus began his usual spiel. "He only eats two times a week…" but he was interrupted by the sounds of gentle footsteps coming down the stairs.

Sharon stood on the bottom step. Her small frame looked gigantic in the proportionately-sized-for-midgets room. Her hair looked brushed, her face had color, and her blue eyes were welcoming.

Andy exclaimed, "You're well! St. Nicholas healed you!"

"The Lord Jesus is gracious," Bishop Nicholas murmured, staring at Sharon as she stared back. She was beautiful, breathtaking. He tried to look away but was captivated. He broke into a broad smile that earned him a smile back.

Just then, two midget boys peeked into the small octagonal window adorned with red leaves to catch a glimpse of Nicholas the healer. When he returned the visual, they ran.

"You'll have to excuse the boys. They are just curious," said Andy, amused. "We've never had a saint visit us before. Come to think of it, we don't get many visitors, especially not famous ones." He poured a cup of peppermint tea for his new guests.

Marcus chuckled, "Oh, you're famous now! Eh, Bishop?"

"Why sure, everyone knows about Saint Nicholas! The town needs a hero," offered Andy.

Nicholas lowered his eyes under the watchful gaze of Sharon.

Marcus finished chewing his bacon, then asked, "What do they say about him?"

"That if his shadow passes over you, God's favor falls on you and you'll be healed of all infirmities, and that blessings will follow you. Some people say that you'll find money in your shoes or socks, or that you'll gain a great fortune."

Nicholas felt a little like he wasn't even in the room, with strangers discussing him.

"Of course, people always confuse material gain with God's blessing," mumbled Marcus.

Harry interrupted, "They say that you brought three kids back to life who were butchered!"

"Isn't it amazing how gossip travels from monks who made a vow of silence?" Nicholas interjected.

"Fishermen claim to see his ghost during tough storms and say that he saves them..." Andy paused, addressing Marcus. He munched on a piece of bacon and continued, addressing the Bishop. "I know that's a little far-fetched, but I have heard about your gifts to the orphans, and how you help the sick and homeless. Everyone in all Asia Minor has heard of it. That's enough to be a hero to me. Are you sure you don't want anything to eat?"

Nicholas shook his head, a little self-conscious.

"Would you prefer fried bugs?" Harry showed him his own plate and crunched off the head of a large, fried beetle.

Marcus looked concerned. "Bishop, you need to eat something. It's been three days since your last meal."

"I'll eat when Asia Minor is under a godly rule."

Nicholas looked at Andy, averting attention from himself.

"So tell me, is everyone like you out here, besides your sister, I mean?"

"Yes. We are orphans, too, you know, when you think about it."

"How? Why? I mean, how'd you end up out here?" asked the fasting fellow.

"Well, years ago we were kicked out of society. We were hunted like deer, used as slaves, made fun of, beaten, locked away, what have you. So we escaped and moved out here together and developed our own community. We're expert craftsmen as you can see. We keep in touch with a few of the outsiders, like the man you stayed with, but for the most part, we live our own lives. We sell our goods to northern Asia and other parts of the world. We don't sell to Rome or any of its people, for fear they may find us out and force us into slavery again."

"How did you know about the man we stayed with?"

Sharon interrupted, "He's our cousin."

"He told us you'd be coming through the forest and to watch out for you—make sure you made it through safely. It took you a long time to get here," offered Andy. He placed a cup of tea on a saucer and passed it to Sharon.

"We had a little trouble along the way. Is that boy still sleeping?" Nicholas remembered Stu, quickly changing the subject.

"It's probably the most comfortable bed he's ever slept in. He's used to sleeping on the streets," Marcus explained. Each person at the table quieted, thinking of such a life, especially at so young of an age.

"I couldn't imagine," Sharon whispered, compassionately.

"You get used to it," Nicholas answered so matter-of-factly.

Sharon gestured for him to be quiet. "That's a horrible thing to say! How would you know?"

"I'm not saying you *should* get used to it, but you do. I've had my share of experiences." Nicholas hesitated. "Stu will be alright. He's a good kid. You know, he'd probably do pretty well up here."

"Well, Andy, you better hide some of that food, too. When he gets up, that boy knows how to eat!" Marcus joked.

Nicholas worked his way up from the floor. "Marcus and I better get prepared. We have a long journey ahead of us."

Marcus handed his plate to Andy as Nicholas walked towards the exit, passing Sharon, briefly nodding, smiling at the newly found color in her cheeks.

"Bishop Nicholas!" Andy shouted.

Nicholas turned around and stopped.

"I know that everyone in our village would be honored if you would speak to us all before you leave... about the things of God? We don't have a man of God to lead us, but we all believe that Jesus is the Christ. And we all know who you are. I know that God could do something in it! Besides, we haven't shown you around the village yet!" Andy proudly snapped on his snow outfit, expecting approval from the Bishop, dismissing any chances of decline.

Chapter 8

Sharon and Andy walked with Marcus, Nicholas, and Stu, showing them around the vanilla village. The snow had finally ceased and the sun kissed the powder covered trees and rooftops of the community, reflecting an amber shimmer, almost too bright for human eyes. The air was still chilly, too chilly for the clothes the trio of men was wearing.

"This place is even more beautiful during the day." Nicholas breathed in, wrapping his arms around himself to keep warm. The crisp air was refreshing, a stark contrast to the bland halls of the monastery.

Sharon brought them to a series of spacious wood and stone buildings with tall, triangular wooden roofs. The angles met and the lines bent, where the roofs peeked out above the entrance, providing a pointed overhang, protecting the front doors and sides from falling snow. They were designed with a strong northern Asian influence. The buildings were identical, except for the markings and statues in the front. As they entered the first one, the trio discovered a world of exotic wood designs; seats with intricately detailed arms and legs, wooden carved couches with velvet cushions, dressers, benches, stools, dining ware, and frames.

An assortment of dwarfs was working on the wood: some were carving, some were sanding, and a few were cutting.

"This is where we make most of our exports," said Sharon, running her finger along the detail of a scenic mahogany carving, admiringly.

"Incredible. I've never seen anything like it!" Nicholas stood in awe.

The dwarfs offered smiles to their visitors and quickly returned to their work.

"We have quite a group of entrepreneurs in our midst," Sharon grinned. "These are all original designs."

They gaped at the beauty of the stunning creations as Nicholas moved into a smaller section of the building, a small room where a dwarf was sanding table legs. Nicholas picked up a wooden staff sitting on a table. It was smooth, stained, and long, but not long enough for a normal-sized man. The tip of the staff was L shaped and curved. "Very nice," he murmured to himself.

The dwarf commented in his high pitched voice, competing with the sound of saws and sanders in the next room, "Oh, that is a defective one—see the way it bends?" He lifted it up to his eye, closed his other eye and looked down the length of it. He then held it up to Nicholas, and Nicholas inspected it himself.

"Amazing."

The boys exited the wood and furniture shop and found their way in front of the next broad building made of stone and wood. Out front was a tall tree laced in fabric. Red velvet bows of many different sizes were attached to the branches, and glass balls were hung strategically around the fir.

Nicholas stopped at the tree and touched a bow, then, a glass ball, inspecting the delicate ornament in awe and wonder.

Sharon noticed Nicholas's curiosity. "Dressing trees is our tradition. Just wait until the Festival of the Christ. You won't recognize this place! We take it very seriously around here!" She took them through the threshold and paused. "This is where we design all of our fabrics." She gave the boys a minute to take it all in. The room was alive with colors, textures, and patterns they'd never seen. The fabrics were rolled on large wooden spools, and many different designs hung from the walls. About a dozen dwarfs were working on looms with the fabric, creating some of the most ornately beautiful tapestries ever witnessed on this side of the world.

"You can touch them!" Sharon offered, rubbing her own hand along one of the fabrics. Different shades of red in a plethora of styles and textures lined the western wall. Marcus rubbed his hand along one of the glimmering, red sheets.

"Amazing, isn't it? It's called silk. It's made from worms found in northern Asia. It's so strong that you can't tear it."

Nicholas took his turn gliding his hand along a furry, velvety, thick burgundy-like fabric with shaggy wool nubs. Sharon caressed the same fabric after him, mimicking his touch—as if she were touching the Bishop's very hand. She shared her thoughts again, "Beautiful, huh? It really keeps a person warm in the winter."

Nicholas glanced at her and smiled. Her eyes were locked on his until she was interrupted by one of the dwarfs.

Sharon led the group into the most incredible room of all. Glass-like tile and marble of all shapes, sizes, and colors consumed the room. There were hundreds of different shades of red, blue, yellow, black, orange, green, and purple. Some of them had swirls with smooth, high gloss textures. Others were solid, rough, or matte finished.

There were baskets all over the floor that were filled with the different colors of the tile, separated by texture and tone for the artist to use. Some of the finished designs hanging on the walls contained tiles that were perfectly broken and placed together in everyday ordinary shapes with incredible detail and structure.

"What an amazing piece of art!" Marcus sighed, eyeing a tile design of snow capped mountains, trees, and a dwarf-designed house in hues of white, green, and red.

Sharon led them through a smaller door in the middle of the building where a dwarf was making blown glass balls, ornaments, and figurines. They were intrigued by the melted glass taking shape around the artist's stick. Beside him was a wood shelf holding many glass creations already complete. Some were in the form of miniature animals, people, and birds.

Nicholas picked up a small figurine no bigger than his thumb and commented, "Impeccable detail! How can someone design something so perfect, yet, so small?"

"Little hands, little designs." Sharon winked.

The Bishop chuckled, remembering where he had heard that comment before.

Stu quickly followed Nicholas's lead and picked up a creature of his own, only to drop it on the ground and watch it shatter into several pieces. He shrieked like a young girl.

Marcus gave the boy a bold stare, scolding him without words.

"What? It was hot!" Stu answered defensively.

Out of nowhere, several dwarfs appeared and confronted Stu. "Be careful. They're hot," one of them said as he bent down to pick up the broken pieces with some sort of contraption. Within a blink of an eye, the two mini men were gone, vanishing through the side door of the factory.

Sharon led them to the last of the three buildings as she exclaimed, "This is our final export!" A frozen fountain made of glass decorated the front of the building, with clear, frosted liquid pouring out of a make-believe faucet, circulating, spiraling down, and into a large bowl.

Stu touched the non-flowing stream. "It's that same stuff we saw in there! It's not real!"

"It's called glass," Sharon corrected him with a giggle. She continued to lead them past the imitation fountain and through the next doorway. "This is my favorite building! I could spend all day in this place!"

"What is it?" asked Nicholas.

"Come see."

The delicious smells were intoxicating as they entered the room. Large pools of sticky goo were spread out in a variety of colors all over the area.

"What is this? Can I drink it?" Stu's mouth watered at the possibilities of tasting this wonderful concoction.

Sharon giggled, "No silly, this is just part of the process. It'll harden and then you can eat it. It's called 'candy.' It's a type of dessert."

At the far side of the room were kettles of thick, dark brown liquid that smelled tantalizing. Sharon dropped in a ladle and pulled some of the liquid out, pouring it into the smooth, round wooden cups beside the pool.

"Try this," she said, as she handed each one of them a full cup.

Stu downed his as a teenage boy would. "That's good," he murmured, trying to salvage any last drop by holding out his tongue and tilting the cup over his face. He didn't even notice the drips that missed his mouth and painted his shirt.

Marcus appeared dreamy, as if he were in Heaven. His eyes shut tight as he sipped the steamy stew. "Mmmmm. That's divine. What is it?" he said, before slurping another mouthful.

"It's called hot chocolate. It's sinfully delicious." Sharon cracked a smile, realizing she was in the presence of a Bishop and a monk. "Uh, bad choice of words. Sorry."

Nicholas chuckled. "I've heard of this. A brother of mine told me about an encounter he had once where he drank this. It tastes even better than he described."

Marcus winced. "What's in this stuff?" He took a few steps forward, noticing a furry beast on all fours in front of him. He closed his eyes and opened them again. Now there were three or four of them.

"Marcus, isn't that what we saw in the forest last night?" asked an amazed and amused Nicholas, trying to discreetly lick the chocolate off his lips.

Stu walked closer to the gazelle wanna-be with tall antlers, fluffy white tail, and beige and white furry patches over its body.

"Be careful, they'll charge if you frighten them," Sharon cautioned Stu. "They're called reindeer." She smiled lovingly at the odd creature.

"I've never seen them before," replied the Bishop.

"That's because they're imported from northern Asia. They were a gift. They decrease our travel time and eliminate the need for horses." Sharon walked over to one of the reindeer and stroked the side of its neck. It turned around and tried to lick her. "They do really well through the mountainous terrain; much better than horses or donkeys. And they're great in the snow." She turned to the furry creature and rubbed its ear and whispered sweetly, "Isn't that right, Blitzen!"

"We, uh, saw one of them last night. It almost looked like it was flying." Marcus looked sheepish.

"That's because it was," answered Sharon with a laugh.

"Really?" asked Stu. "Are you joking with us?"

She gave a crooked grin, "Of course...*not*. But if you watch them run up the mountains, it's amazing. They glide across the rocks. They're so fast! It can look like they truly are flying! You probably saw Dasher. He gets a charge dashing up the rocks in front of people. That's where he gets his name."

Sharon led them to a snow covered meadow where several of the reindeer were playing.

"Don't you worry about them running off to warmer climates? Marcus wondered aloud.

She turned around and looked at him with a smile. "They love it here. They like the colder weather. Besides, we feed them quite well. They're not going to pass up a free meal. We're family."

"This family's getting stranger all the time," Stu joked, shortly before Nicholas nudged him with his elbow in an attempt to shut the boy up.

Nicholas sat near the open fire with more than a hundred dwarfs facing him. He gazed upon their friendly little faces. They were quiet, staring intently back at him.

"Dear friends...may I call you that? How about brothers? The Bible says that when we believe in the Lord Jesus Christ, we are all brothers in the Lord. You are my brother, and my sister, if you believe, no matter how big or small you are."

A cheery chuckle swept through the crowd.

He continued,"...and all of us—yes, all of us—fall short of the glory of God. It is by Christ we have been saved, through his sacrifice on the cross. Not by works, not by how good someone is, not by what kind of trade he or she has, or what he does or doesn't do; but by grace, we find salvation. The Bible says there is none good; not a one. I am a sinner. But by God's grace I am forgiven, and you are too."

Nicholas preached for quite a while. The fading sun was already dimming her light and the fire lowered her rage to a light hum with occasional whistles and crackles, while dwarfs fed her new wood to burn every thirty minutes or so.

Nicholas continued, "The apostle Paul said that he will show you man's faith by his works. If we love Jesus, as we say we do, then we will want to do the things he does: to reach out to the orphans, the widows, those less fortunate than ourselves. That is the true gift of God—to take the gift that we possess, and use it to bless others in the name of Christ. I will ask you, what is it that you possess? What talent or gift do you have that you can share to multiply God's kingdom? Perhaps you are a cook? Perhaps you are a good listener? I've seen amazing things while I've been here. It's obvious you've already learned to share your talents with each other. Now, how about to the unlovable? How about to the forgotten or mistreated?"

Resting at a wooden table near the reformed fire, Nicholas and Marcus made small talk with several of the dwarfs. The platinum moon gave her light where the fire fell short. A boar roasted on a long stick by a smaller fire, sure to be the night's meal. Nicholas was easily distracted by the loud, live music, the dancing, the yelps of joy, but most of all, by the way Sharon, the beautiful young woman whom God healed the night before, kept looking at him. He hoped that she didn't notice the many times he was looking back at her, too. It was unruly behavior for a Bishop to even consider a woman's beauty, knowing he could never have any type of God-given relationship with her.

"AAAaaaaaahhhh!" yelled a husky but short dwarf who fell in the fire during a courageous little dance.

The scream broke Nicholas out of his trance.

"Saint Nicholas! We need your help!" screamed Andy, desperately.

The Bishop rushed over to the hurting little fellow and discovered third degree burns on his arm and part of his leg. It was obvious by the man's face that he was in tremendous pain.

"Can you heal him?" questioned Andy, nervously.

"God does the healing. Someone go get some cool water, quickly! And get some rags! Marcus, where's Stu?"

"I don't know. Dancing, I think!"

"I need you to get my small pouch and bring it here!"

While one of the dwarfs ran off to fetch the supplies, Nicholas began to pray, "Dear Lord, please heal this young man! Touch his arm and leg, healing it in your name. Please take away the burn and the pain..."

The man first opened his right eye, then his left, as if he was expecting magic to heal his arm before his very eyes.

"Is it healed?" asked an impatient Andy.

"Nothin'," said the ailing little man, as he looked down at his burns.

Nicholas patted him on the shoulder. "Give it time. Even if God doesn't heal it, he gave us the brains and abilities to take care of your wounds."

Marcus returned with the black pouch and Nicholas opened it, pulling out a few swamp willow leaves and a piece of aloe plant. He broke the cold, green, aloe leaf in half and smeared the gooey green substance onto the miniature man's wounds.

"Aaahh..." the man winced, "it's cold."

"It'll soothe your burns and make it heal quicker... Here, suck on these leaves. They contain an ingredient called aspirin. It's mild, but it will take away the pain for a short time. Here are a few more to take with you," Nicholas instructed, as he handed the man the long green leaves, foreign to their region.

Andy pleaded, "Bishop, please stay another night. It's dangerous to travel this late. You will be well rested in the morning, and I'll have Sharon cook a wonderful meal for you."

"Only if it contains hot chocolate and one of those round things again. What did you call them?" Nicholas replied, half jokingly.

"Oh, you mean the cookie? Yes, those are good."

Darkness. Flames consuming homes, churches, and lives. Screams. Men of God pulled out of their bed during the night and beaten, tortured, and murdered. Monasteries in madness. Cries and wails of the innocent.

The morning light peeked through the mountains and flooded the village, permeating the darkness, awaking the slumbering souls who partied too much and too late the night before. Slowly opening his eyes, Nicholas yawned, stretched, and thanked the Lord for a beautiful day. He was bundled under a furry green blanket given to him by an admiring seamstress the night before. He glanced over to see Marcus and Stu still sleeping, then to the front of the room, spying the three presents that awaited them. He adjusted his eyes, pulled back the covers and quietly made his way over to the three bundles of clothes: blue, brown, and burgundy. He found the one labeled for him and humored himself by slipping it on.

"I see it fits," said a pleased Andy, as Nicholas entered the lavender and white cheery kitchen. He had never seen painted walls like that before, and found it warm and inviting.

Sharon turned around from cooking and inspected Nicholas from head to toe. "It looks good on you. It's the fabric I saw you touching yesterday."

"I noticed," said Nicholas appreciatively, with a grin.

"Plus, it matches that ol' sack you carry around."

The deep reddish burgundy coat with the shaggy wool nubs fit perfectly. It was trimmed in a beautiful white soft plush wool material, about three inches wide, and two inches thick. He was given a stocking cap to match, and black leather mittens to keep his hands warm.

"I've never seen these before," he said, holding up the mittens, acknowledging the big compartment that held all four fingers, with the thumb separated.

"They're a necessity around here. You'll like them. Try them on," encouraged Andy.

"I see you found your gifts?" said Nicholas, laughing a little at Marcus's new style as he entered the room, wearing the brown and black, crushed velvet outfit that was very similar to his own.

"What? You don't think it fits?" humored Marcus as he rubbed his hand along the material down his chest to his waist, resting his thumb on the thick black belt.

Sharon gave him a big smile. "You look lovely!"

Three knocks echoed through the door. Andy briskly walked over to it and cracked it open. Young Will, a small and anxious dwarf dressed in all furry blue and a white winter's cap, stood at the door and anxiously pushed his way in.

"Andy, the Bishop can't leave today! We've gotten word that Diocletian has soldiers all over the local towns looking for the one they call Saint Nicholas, the healer. He's arrested several Christians and burned down a number of churches."

Nicholas countered, "I appreciate your concern, but if the Lord wanted me to stay, he'd let me know. Have faith, my friends."

"You're welcome to stay as long as you like. You are safe here, and everyone loves you," Andy offered, hoping the Bishop would change his mind.

Silence.

"Will you offer communion to us before you leave, Bishop?" questioned a hopeful, jolly Andy.

"At the last supper, Jesus took a cup filled with dark wine and told his disciples, 'This is my blood of the new covenant, which will be poured out for you. Drink it…'"

Nicholas dipped the silver chalice into the big silver bowl of red wine, Rome's finest he was told by Harry, and held the cup as the dwarfs came one by one to drink from it. He refilled the cup as needed until the entire village had taken communion.

Then, holding up an unleavened loaf of bread, Nicholas blessed it and broke it in half. "This is the body of Christ, which he gave for you. Eat it…and remember his sacrifice." He passed the bread and everyone in the village broke off a piece of it. He could tell by some of their faces that this was their first communion. He delighted in that. It was a sacred moment that was often tainted by repetition and remote traditionalism.

As customary by religious law, viewing the blood and flesh as truly sacred and holy, the acting bishop or priest who offered the elements for communion must drink and eat anything left over. Nicholas knew he couldn't finish the leftover bowl of wine he had blessed alone, so he offered some to Marcus, another qualified man of the cloth. Of course, Stu volunteered to help drink the wine but the Bishop rejected his offer.

The two men sat in the chill of the day under a naked tree and drank, drank, and drank some more, until the elements were entirely gone.

Stu approached the inebriated brothers. He was wearing a blue furry suit and cap, similar to the outfit Will was wearing earlier that morning. He looked like a stiff little blue fur ball.

Marcus burst out laughing. "Gee, little feller, you sure grew quickly since this morning!" Marcus slurred, confusing Stu for an overgrown Will.

"Marcus, where's your manners? He's not taller, we're just smaller!" Nicholas laughed at himself.

Stu was a little upset. "C'mon guys, we have to get out of here, back to normal-ville... You know—normal civilization where the doorways are big enough to stand in?"

Nicholas tried to get up and stumbled a bit. Marcus got up and tried to help him, but he too stumbled in the snow, falling to his knees and laughing as he pulled down Bishop Nicholas with him.

Firm hands grabbed a hold of the Bishop and helped him to his feet. The hands felt warm and gentle on his side and arm. They tingled his body. He turned around to see Sharon standing behind him, helping him, holding him.

Stu grabbed Marcus and helped walk him towards the cottage.

"I don't think they're going anywhere today, Stu. Why don't you take Marcus to his room to lie down?" Sharon suggested.

The so-called Saint, inebriated and vulnerable, connected eyes with Sharon. His walls were down and the scared little boy inside was revealed. He didn't have to say anything. Sharon could see it and feel it. "I love you," he spoke softly, smiling with a gentle smile as if he was talking to his mother who had passed when he was just a child. Sharon thought it was the wine talking and just sighed briefly as the two walked together. She led him to the thick of the woods where they could talk a little more privately, and he could avoid the stares and judgment of the dwarfs. "So why are you here? You don't really fit in," slurred a concerned, curious Nicholas.

"I fit in here more than I do down there in the city." She took a few more steps before proceeding, "I don't know. I've been there. I lived with my cousin a while, but, I just didn't like it." She looked up at the sky peering through the trees. "I feel God up here. Kinda like when Moses went up the mountain to be with God. Can't you sense him here?" She smiled with a faraway look on her face, blossoming with childlike wonder.

Nicholas stared at her. She was just lovely. "Yeah, but eventually Moses had to come down. The people needed him. And God needed him to help the people."

Sharon took a breath to let it sink in. "Up here everyone is friendly. They are amazing. Besides, they're family, *real* family. Andy took care of me after Mom and Dad died."

"How old were you when they died?"

"I don't know. I sort of blocked it out. I was a lot shorter than Andy and Harry though," she laughed. "When I kept growing, I was upset. I wanted to be little like everyone else." She offered him a flirtatious smile.

Nicholas didn't realize when the change happened, but Sharon stopped holding him up and was now holding his hand. He felt her heart pulsating through her warm fingers and against his. They had been talking for what appeared to be hours and the sun was setting beneath the south side of the cold mountain terrain once again.

"We better get back to the village before the sun fades," Sharon warned, moving closer to Nicholas, so close that they were practically touching. The evening chill set in and the wind pushed its way through the fabric covering their bodies. She shivered. Nicholas pulled her closer. She stared at his lips. Her eyes were dreamy. *This doesn't make sense*, she thought to herself. She knew him a mere two days and already she had fallen madly in love.

He stared at her long hair that poked itself from beneath her white cap and had turned to a fiery colored frizz in the winter's wind. It was beautiful. She was beautiful. He was a *man of God*, he kept thinking to himself. How could he be here? How could he want this? But he did. He wanted it, and he wanted it badly.

He studied every part of her face as she talked; her rosy cheeks, her deep set eyes, her high cheek bones and soft milky skin, and was now fixated on her tender, moist lips that encircled her warm breath. He wanted to feel them, to touch them. He wanted to kiss them. He imagined it, but knew he couldn't do it. It could mean his job, his role in life, his existence as a Bishop, his respect in the community.

He quickly glanced away, avoiding the temptation, gazing at the beautiful mistletoe growing around him. He breathed deeply, unable to come up with anything to say, and their eyes met once again. She leaned in and he stood there, his heart pounding like the sound of a hundred horses going into battle. If the horses were coming against him, they were winning. He was falling. Nicholas closed his eyes and leaned forward. He could almost feel her breath on his face, her lips so close and...

"Sharon... There you two are!" said the little voice coming from four foot Harry, oblivious to the pursuing intimacy between them.

Fire.   Swords thrusting and slicing.   Children screaming. Buildings burning.

Nicholas slept that night better than he had in years. He slept so hard and long that he didn't even notice the sun gracing his room through the window like he usually did. He didn't wake up from the smell of warm fried foods permeating the house either, or to the laughter from Andy, Marcus, and Stu as they ate a delicious breakfast.

He dreamed of the last evening's temptation. Except in his dreams, the kiss wouldn't have been a sin, and there would be no penalty. Could such a place exist? Could a man of God ever marry? Could he be held in the arms of a comforter, other than the Holy Spirit? Is it blasphemy, he wondered, to even ponder such thoughts?!

Cardinal Michaels appeared in the forefront of his mind. Nicholas jumped out of bed and out of slumber. He was gasping for breath.

Stu stepped out of the cottage style house and onto the soft snow to find the entire town gathered to say their goodbyes. Marcus and Nicholas followed him. Whispers echoed through the crowd until Harry stepped forward and approached the Bishop.

"Saint Nicholas, we made you a present for you to remember us by."

One of the wood-working dwarfs stepped forward and handed Nicholas a beautifully designed and decorated wooden staff: one that would actually fit an average sized human being. The handle of the staff was oval shaped, adorned with green and red translucent stones. The rest of the staff was layered with smaller gems.

Nicholas picked it up, admiringly looked at it, twirled it, and placed it down again. "This is beautiful! Thank you so very much, all of you." His eyes skimmed the crowd, but he didn't see his crush, Sharon.

Andy approached him. "Saint Nicholas, as a community, we thought about what you said yesterday, and we want to help with your mission. We're professional craftsmen with plenty of time on our hands, and plenty of wood too. We'd like to make toys and gifts for the orphans."

Nicholas was overwhelmed with joy. His rosy cheeks and nose were bursting with an accompanying explosive smile.

"I knew God brought me here for a reason!" he crowed with overbearing excitement.

Harry matched Nicholas's enthusiasm and responded, "Well, we better get started!"

The trio of friends who appeared as giants to the dwarfs knelt down and hugged several of the villagers and was guided to a beautiful red sleigh attached to a pair of the reindeer.

"I'm going to take you guys to the bottom of the mountain," informed Harry, graciously.

They thanked Andy and Harry for their hospitality. Stu tossed the trio's bags into the back of the sleigh before climbing in himself. With a snap of the rein, the reindeer began to move quickly out of the vanilla village and down the slope, dodging barren trees and thick packs of snow. Nicholas turned around for a final view of the beautiful winter wonderland community, waving to most of his newly-found friends.

Chapter 9

By now, Gabriella, our hopeless romantic, was dreamy-eyed and giggly at the story of the budding romance between Nicholas and Sharon.

"Is she a princess, Daddy?" questioned Makayla, leaning her head against my chest and looking up at me with her chocolate puppy eyes.

"I guess you could say she was! Just like you, Gabriella, and Elisha! You are *my* princesses."

Not everyone likes a princess story. I was reminded of this by the young visitors that made their way into the living room and sat on the couch across from me. They had been there for a good part of the story, and so far were not impressed by little dwarfs, a winter wonderland village, or a mushy love story.

"How about a pirate story?" exclaimed Jackson, holding a newly opened pirate toy.

"A pirate story?"

"Yeah! With fighting and stuff!"

"This is the story of Santa Claus!" I reminded him.

"Well, tell a scary story!"

Ah, the desires of a four-year-old boy. "Hmm... Well, hang on, Jackson. Keep listening. I think you may like it," I said with a wink. I wasn't used to sharing stories with boys. It was easy to tell a love story to three little girls and make them melt—especially if it involved a fairy tale with a prince and living happily ever after.

Aunt Lori had arrived with her three sons a half hour earlier. Uncle Mike was away at a conference, and wouldn't be home until Christmas night. While Jackson and Calvin sat on the couch listening to the story, Lori placed Parker on the floor and he crawled his way from the kitchen and into the living room, stopping at my feet and trying to climb my legs.

I could hear my wife, Nicole, and my sister, Lori, discussing babies in the kitchen as they finished the last preparations of the meal. I was distracted by the scrumptious smell.

"What happened next, Daddy?" little Makayla reminded me that we weren't even close to finishing the story.

"Hmmm..." I took a sip of my drink and closed my eyes. "Where was I?"

...It was dusk when the trio finally reached Myra. The sky was overcast, and the moon trickled just enough light to see that the town appeared abandoned.

They approached the monastery. Even in the dark, they could see the black stains that marked the once beautiful beige and white, stone and clay structure.

Nicholas ran inside to find it empty of souls, and the sanctuary in shambles, still burning. The walls were charred, books were burned, and tables were broken. He walked through the rubble and knelt at the altar, his chest heaving as tears streamed down his face, stricken with grief.

Marcus stood silently and watched from the back of the sanctuary, slowly picking up a burned scroll. He glanced quickly at Stu, who didn't seem to know how or what to feel.

The winds picked up, slicing through their clothes, and Stu found a little corner of the wall without debris to sit down and rest, hiding him from the cold. Within minutes, the tear stained Saint walked by and gently touched Stu's shoulder, continuously inspecting his home.

"Does that stuff really work?" Stu interrupted him from his inspection.

"Does what work?" Nicholas sighed.

"Prayer... I see you do it all the time."

"Silly boy," the Bishop said with a sniff and a faint chuckle, "you've seen God move more in a few days than most people see in a lifetime. You tell me, does prayer work? I'll keep praying, and you keep watching. No, better yet, why don't you start praying, too. The need for intercession is greater than ever." With that, Nicholas lifted his hand off Stu's shoulder and continued to walk past him and into what used to be an adjacent room, currently separated by just a few feet of rubble.

Meanwhile, Diocletian and his men victoriously rode from village to village, daring anyone to confess Christ, and beating, killing, or torturing those who did. He burned down churches and arrested the monks and bishops. Each victimized village would suffer greater than the last, keeping with the strokes of Diocletian's ego.

One thing continued to escape him though: the arrest and murder of the great Saint Nicholas from Myra. What started out as curiosity about a man who *heals* became an obsession, and Diocletian wouldn't stop until his quest was successful. He was intrigued by the tales, and thought about the status he'd acquire by capturing the famous Bishop. He had plans to discredit Nicholas's good name and the false God he served once he was terminated.

Only one man deserves that kind of attention, Diocletian thought. *Me.*

"So what now?" asked Marcus tentatively, in a soft, broken voice.

"We'll make our way to Patara." Nicholas bent over amid the rubble in what used to be his office, turned over a few pieces of burnt wood and some scrolls on the floor to discover his wooden cross, still intact. It was the very cross he used to wear from his cloak as a monk in Patara. He picked up the cross and rubbed it as he used to, his thumb stroking the top back and forth. "…If Patara is still standing."

The two men and their teenage companion traveled to the coast. The silver moon glistened off the crystal blue ocean, giving the only light for the weary travelers.

The trio could see fire further down the beach and they heard the sounds of fishermen talking and feasting, probably preparing for a night of catching oysters.

They also heard what sounded like horses' hooves approaching above them, as they made their way to the bottom of the beachside cliffs.

Nicholas put his finger over his mouth to silence Marcus and Stu, but it was too late.

"Hey! You! Halt!" commanded the Roman soldier, pointing his finger accusingly at Nicholas and his companions. The trio fled, picking up speed as they reached the bottom of the grassy and stone crag. "I said Haaalt!" the voice crowed again with the authority of Rome behind it. Half a dozen Roman soldiers galloped their horses east a few hundred yards to a path that would lead them down the rocky face and to the ocean.

"Great! What now?" huffed Marcus as he ran behind his mentor, losing his breath.

"Hurry, to the tombs!" directed Nicholas, pointing to what appeared to be miniature, detailed stone houses with columned entrances carved into the west side of the cliff, and ornamented with boiseries, stone and marble. These were the graves of the wealthy, and rightly so.

As they reached the bottom of the west side cliffs and began their climb, the Roman soldiers finally reached the sand a few hundred yards away to the east.

In a cautious whisper, Nicholas commanded, "Quickly, into one of the catacombs!"

Stu emphatically shook his head. "Are you crazy? I think I'm safer with the soldiers!"

"If they catch you, you'll have one of these tombs as your very own," interrupted Marcus.

Nicholas laughed sarcastically, "Nah, he could never afford one of these... That one!" Nicholas told Stu, pointing to a creepy looking crevice in the rocks, much older, smaller, and worn than most of the tombs. "They won't look for you there. Go!"

"What? I want to go with you!" The young teen's eyes begged of fear.

"No, boy, we'll be safer if we split up."

In the meantime, Marcus found his way into a sturdy stone crypt a little bit above and to the right of Stu's, and watched the soldiers through a crack.

Nicholas climbed his way to a higher level and crawled into a large tomb with three stone columns at its entrance. The tomb was too dark to see anything, but this didn't hinder him from feeling his way to the back, past the two chilling stone compartments holding cadavers and leaning against the cold rear wall. He rested his head on one of the stone coffins, nearly out of breath, as he heard the Roman soldiers getting closer.

"Where'd they go?"

"In the tombs!" a soldier replied.

The commander snorted, "Why not? They're all dead men anyway. Go get them!"

"I'm not going in there! You go in there!" retorted one of his men.

"They'll be out soon enough!" the smug commander replied, resting on his horse and chewing on his nails.

The soldiers quieted down long enough for Stu to think they were gone. The frightfully isolated juvenile crept out of the tomb in search of his friends.

"There's one!" shouted the heavy-set soldier, as he tried to corner Stu.

Nicholas couldn't see what was going on, but he could tell by the excited voices that Stu had been caught. Satisfied with the capture, the soldiers made their way to another location.

The Bishop felt around the right side of him. His hands stopped at a loose, cold brick sticking partially out of the wall, and with a slight tug, he pulled it free. He stuck his hand in the hole he had made and pulled out a few coins, then, returned the brick. He leaned his head back down against the stone coffin, affectionately touching it with his left hand, while fumbling with the coins.

"Mom, Dad…I miss you," he said, as tears seeped from his eyes.

Hours had passed and Nicholas made his way out of his parents' tomb to a breathtaking view. The oversized platinum moon now sat upon the waters. Tendrils of light danced with the current and reflected on his face and the entrances to the death caves. He made his way down to the beach where Marcus was sitting by the water, staring out at the sea.

Nicholas stood behind him and placed his hand on Marcus's shoulder. The moonlight gleamed in the reflection of Marcus's tears streaming down his face.

"I don't want to do this anymore. I'm scared, and I'm tired of running." His mouth was quivering.

"Marcus, God is with us."

"Is he really?" he blurted in frustration. "What about the rest of the monks from Myra? What about them?"

"Being a Christian isn't about our freedom here on Earth. It's about our freedom in Heaven, and *being free* spiritually. Have faith, my friend. You have a heavenly Father who loves you and is taking care of you. Can't you see he's been with us all along?" Nicholas pleaded, with his own tears expelled for Marcus. A wisp of fear and doubt tried to force its way into the Bishop's mind and heart, but he shoved it away.

The distant fire glowed faintly as the voices of the fishermen-turned gamblers carried up the coast.

Marcus and Nicholas were sitting side by side on the beach, glancing at the man-made light occasionally, while discussing a plan. "We need a boat to get across. That's the safest way to Patara," Nicholas reasoned.

"Great! How about we ask our dwarf friends to come whittle us a boat out of all this wood?" Marcus said sarcastically, releasing his grief to a lighthearted laugh.

The two men of God made their way up the peaceful, lulling shore to the boat docks. Several fishermen were sitting around a dead tree stump, drinking and gambling with homemade cards and stones. The fishermen didn't even notice Marcus and Nicholas standing there. They were either too caught up in the intensity of their game, or too drunk to care.

"Stu, what are you doing here?" said a surprised Marcus, wondering how the young lad escaped from the Roman soldiers and ended up at the gamblers' table.

Stu found himself in the 4th seat of the group, trying his luck at a few games. He glanced at Marcus and back at his cards, as if his eyes were saying, "How dare you break my concentration!" He tugged at his lip and placed his cards down for his challengers to see.

"A-ha! You are mine now, boy!" shouted the scraggly fisherman who was missing most of his teeth. "You're mine!" he growled again.

Nicholas could see the fear in Stu's eyes. Assuming he was the captain of the tiny fishing boat, Nicholas addressed the grimy, wild-haired drunk. "We need a boat ride to Patara."

"Why don't you walk? It's easier," murmured one of the drunken fishermen.

"We need a boat," Nicholas persisted, tossing a coin at the toothless man. "Will this do for the three of us?"

"This boy ain't goin' nowhere. He's my slave for the rest of the season." The drunken fisherman looked at the coin. "And I ain't givin' no boat ride in the night," he said simply, shuffling the cards to start a new game.

"How much will it take to have you take us?"

"You can buy my boat for all I care, but I don't sail at night, especially this time of year."

Nicholas looked at Stu. "C'mon, it's time to go."

The drunkard stood up and aggressively put his hand in front of the boy. "Did you hear what I said? That boy ain't goin' nowhere."

Nicholas took Stu's arm to remove him from harm's way and the kidnapping fisherman tried to grab Nicholas's hand with one hand, while attempting to punch him with the other. The Bishop blocked the punch and placed his cane between the man's legs and slightly behind the left one, gave him a slight push, and the off-duty fisherman found himself off balance and lying flat on the sand. Nicholas placed the tip of his cane against the man's chest, as if he were a pirate with a sword, threatening the fisherman's life.

"That coin should pay for the boy's debt," commanded Nicholas to the fallen fisherman.

"What do we do now?" asked an unsure Marcus again, constantly seeking direction from his Bishop.

"We go fishing," smirked Nicholas.

"Fishing?"

The Bishop tossed a second coin into the defeated man's lap. "We need a net."

Stu stuck the captured small fish with wooden sticks through their mouths and out the side of their tails. He handed one to Nicholas and kept one for himself. They held the fish over their open fire to cook while Marcus continued to cast his net.

"Guys! I can't do this! It's been at least a half hour and I haven't caught anything!"

The Bishop took a bite. "Are you praying, Brother Marcus?"

"Yes."

"Pray harder," Nicholas said humorously.

Just then Marcus found himself splashing and thrashing around in the knee-deep water, fighting what appeared to be a massive fish. He dragged it to shore.

"Ya got something?" Nicholas said with his mouth full, not even looking at Marcus.

"It's huge! It weighs a ton!" Marcus pulled the net onto the shore to discover an oversized brown and white puffer fish, puffed up like a balloon with its spikes showing for a fight.

Stu informed him, "You know you can't eat those!"

Nicholas and Stu both laughed.

"What now?" asked a wearied Marcus, realizing his constant repetition of the question.

"You're going to stop asking me 'what now' and start making your own decisions," Nicholas answered like a schoolteacher. He walked over to the pregnant looking fish gasping for water and cut its belly open with his stick. Twenty gold coins poured out of it.

"Wow," Marcus and Stu breathed in unison as they stood over the deflated and bloodied fish.

Nicholas poured the gold coins covered in crimson fish guts onto the fisherman's lap, who was still sulking over his loss of a boy slave. The dirty old man looked up at Nicholas in wonder.

"For your boat," said the Bishop.

The boat wasn't much to look at. The wooden structure had seen much better days, and was only big enough for the three of them. It wobbled through the water precariously, escaping promises of a safe journey.

"I'm captain of the sea!" yelled Stu, like a boy playing pirate as he and his two companions made their way out to the black waters of the Mediterranean.

"Ever steered a boat before?" asked Marcus.

"In my dreams! I was made for sailing! And I'm unstoppable! Ha ha!"

"Looks like we've got a real pirate on our hands!" Nicholas sarcastically addressed Marcus.

"The most frightful pirate of the Mediterranean!" an arrogant, playful Stu answered.

"Well, Mr. Captain, king of the sea, I mean, Mr. dreadful pirate, it appears you have us going in the wrong direction. Keep us parallel with the land – and make sure the land is on our right side. We need to go west."

The waters were choppy. The trip was long and exhausting. The ocean breeze was biting. Stu hung over the bow of the boat vomiting his early morning snack, as he did three previous times in the past hour. His face was pale green and he could barely move.

"Oh mighty captain, still feeding them fish, eh?" Marcus laughed at him as he continued to row.

"Keep your eyes on the horizon," suggested Nicholas.

The waves rocked the small fishing boat continuously, as the sky secreted heavy dew upon their heads. Thunder shook the air from all around as dark clouds crashed into one another.

"I'd look at it, if I could find it!" answered Stu, just before releasing some more of his fish dinner.

He was shivering. They all were. Marcus continued to row, despite his coughing and inability to see anything around him. Heavy rains and rough seas were synonymous with the Fall season. Stu leaned out a little too far as the boat was making its way over a wave. The liquid mountain tossed the vessel enough to force Stu out and into the black abyss.

"Stu! Stu!" Marcus yelled, peering into the deep black sea that engulfed him.

The quick flashes of lightning gave Nicholas enough time to spot the youngster's head a few feet away.

"There he is, to your right!" he yelled.

Marcus tried to steer the boat in Stu's direction, but the unforgiving wind and rain fought him with every paddle.

"Stu!"

Stu's head was going under, and the men watched helplessly as they were forced into another direction.

"Lord, Jesus, please stop this wind and rain. Help us save this young boy's life!" cried Nicholas.

Marcus managed to navigate the boat towards Stu again. The rain felt like bullets on his face. Nicholas dove into the icy water, waiting for God's cue with the lightning as he treaded.

Cloud against Cloud. *Crackle!* There it was! Starting from the west and stretching across the sky to the east, the lightning flash lasted longer than any other bolt of the evening. Nicholas spotted Stu a few feet away, his head bobbing above and below the surface. He swam out to the boy, treaded with his head above the water, put his arm around Stu's chest, and dragged him to the boat. Marcus helped pull the lad over the edge of the boat, and the young man flopped on the floor of the vessel like a fish. Nicholas quickly covered him with his robe to keep him warm. Stu coughed and gasped, his cold breath spewing vaporous clouds.

The frosty rains finally ceased and the dancing sun played chase with the boys on the water from the east as they approached Patara. It was a long night, and the men welcomed morning. They were able to get onto the shore, past the cliffs, and through the thick of the city before the blazing rays of light caught up with them.

As they reached the top of the hill that faced the monastery in Patara, they were delighted to see it still intact on the other side of the valley. Marcus eagerly ran with all his might through the meadow towards the building, screaming, "Praise God!"

Chapter 10

"It's good to see you again," faked the Cardinal, as he stood in the doorway to Nicholas's room.

Wearing clean, white undergarments and drying his wet hair with a cloth, Nicholas spoke aloud his fears. "What happened to the orphanage?"

The Cardinal shifted his eyes. "It was moved to another location: a place more suitable for children."

"Who takes care of them?" Nicholas's lips thinned and he felt his anger surfacing, recognizing the cover-up language of the Cardinal, a language he had heard too many times before.

"It's run by the government, more or less. A few sisters still work with them," he responded in an offhanded manner. "Listen, several other Bishops in the territory are making their way to Patara. We'll have an emergency council this evening. I expect to see you there." The Cardinal quickly exited, hoping to avoid any more questions.

The bloodied sky was cradled by the hillside above the monastery. Although it appeared warm, the air remained wet and chilly. The Cardinal, Bishop St. Claire, Bishop Nicholas, Bishop Bartholomew, and Bishop Mattias, stood in a semi-circle to intently discuss their strategy to protect themselves and their monasteries from the persecution of Diocletian.

"…We must take whatever measures are necessary to ensure safety!" said Mattias with enthusiasm and conviction…

"Like getting rid of the orphans?" Nicholas challenged him. Nicholas was all too familiar with Mattias. He was all about tradition, a slave to religious ritual, and his identity was hidden by his title and flowing red robe. He loved the attention he received in public, but had no clue as to how to love others and touch lives for Christ. He was constantly trying to invent some form of addition to include in the rituals of the church, hoping to make a name for himself, as if that would give him more favor with God, or the Cardinal.

"Yes! We made the right decision in that, and don't you question it. The government would have used the kids as an excuse to control the monasteries." Mattias realized that Nicholas succeeded fishing for more information and quickly silenced himself before getting in trouble with the Cardinal.

"Whose safety are we ensuring?" Nicholas shot back at him. "What about the children? What happens to them now?"

The gentle, tenderhearted Bishop St. Claire interjected. "I've heard a nasty rumor that Diocletian is developing a rare army from these orphans. They're training for battle as babies."

"Look, we had to do what was best for the monastery. We must ensure the safety of our brothers first. We can't give Diocletian a reason to destroy us," repeated Mattias, in a futile effort to rephrase his words and sound less harsh.

"Interesting. I thought our brothers were called to surrender their lives for the sake of the gospel. We should ask them why they joined in the first place. Isn't our primary purpose to share the gospel of Christ with the hurting and the lost? Not protect a building by sacrificing children!" Nicholas was growing in passion as they volleyed back and forth about the welfare of the orphans.

"Your monastery is burned to the ground. Don't encourage the destruction of ours," responded the Cardinal. "Perhaps if you learned submission you wouldn't be in the trouble you are today."

"What trouble is that?" asked Nicholas.

"We all know there's a hefty price on your head. You still haven't learned to work with the system," threatened the Cardinal. He stared down his nose at the Bishop as Nicholas matched his steady gaze.

"The system was made by man. I answer to no one but my God." Nicholas spoke with a low growl through clenched teeth.

"I'll be sure to convey that message to the Archbishop," smirked the sarcastic Cardinal.

Bishop Mattias continued. "We need to change with modern times. If we learn to work with Diocletian, maybe…"

"Work with him?" interrupted a hot-tempered Nicholas, his passion at full force now, exposed through his bright red face. "He kidnaps children to build armies, murders our brothers and sisters in the Lord, burns down our churches and monasteries, and you suggest we work with him?"

Spurred on by the Cardinal's verbal attack on Nicholas, Mattias sarcastically returned, "Most of those children were nothing more than street rats, a byproduct of their adulterous, sinful parents. We couldn't help them. Most of them would have turned back to the streets anyway. You know it's true. So don't feel badly for them. They'll never amount to anything. We need to…"

Before Mattias could finish his sentence, he felt a fast fist thrusting into his jaw, knocking him off balance and forcing him on the ground. Nicholas stood over him, his fist still clenched. Bishops St. Claire and Bartholomew grabbed onto Nicholas's robe to protect Mattias from further blows. Nicholas jerked his arms back from the two and walked away from the council. All of the Bishops were stunned into silence.

Meanwhile, Marcus and Stu shared the wild tales of their adventures together with the rest of the monks at Patara. Marcus had become somewhat of a legend to them by now.

The Cardinal and Bishop Bartholomew walked in on the congregation of brown skirted men to find them encircled around the boy, with Marcus's hand on his shoulder. Stu was crying. Marcus finished the prayer, and lifted his head to see his superiors standing over them.

"He's one of us, now!" Marcus exclaimed.

The scent of fresh vegetable soup escaped the kitchen and permeated his senses. However, as hungry as he was, Nicholas refused to eat, spending the evening on his knees, deep in intimacy with the Father, Almighty God. He had been on the road so much lately that the calluses on his knees were wearing off and blood began to seep through his skin and undergarments from rubbing on the hard clay and brick floor the last few hours. His old room even had indentions on the floor in certain locations from his all day and night prayer sessions as a young monk. This night would be no exception.

He knew that sound. It was almost spiritual. He felt the presence, and although he was nervous, he was prepared.

Cardinal St. Michaels walked in the room. "I have informed the Archbishop of your situation and your expulsion as Bishop. In the morning you will remove yourself from this monastery. You are no longer in service to the Lord."

"I will always be in service to the Lord, with or without the red suit."

The Cardinal looked bemused, then, without a response, removed himself from Nicholas's room. Nicholas returned to his bloodied knee position.

Nicholas had fallen into what he thought was a trance. He saw what appeared to be his future. There were hundreds of thousands of people calling out to him, blessing him, crying to him. He was trying to tell them about Jesus, the Christ, the Son of the living God, but they weren't listening. Their cries got louder and louder and louder until...

Thump! Thump! Thump!

Nicholas returned to the present, breathless and startled.

"You are under arrest!" barked one of the Roman soldiers towering over him. Nicholas slowly stood up without a fight. A second Roman soldier placed braces around Nicholas's wrists.

Cardinal St. Michaels watched smugly from the inside of the window as the soldiers took Nicholas away.

Bishop Bartholomew was in tears. "I can't believe you did that to him! I can't believe you did that to him!" His voice rose with a tremble, as he questioned the Cardinal verbally for the first time in his career as a Bishop.

"I did what was best for the monastery. Did you want yours to burn down like the others? He's a big target. It was an easy trade," the Cardinal simpered.

Chapter 11

Byzantium's prison was nicknamed "the underground grave for the living" because most of the people who were imprisoned there never made it out. It was an ancient dungeon, with moist, insect-infested dirt floors and walls, supported by lumps of clay where handcuffs and ankle cuffs were occasionally connected. The smell was unimaginable, reeking from years of sewage, no sunlight, and constant body odor.

Nicholas was tossed down the stairs, picked up again, and slammed against the wall several times where chains were then shackled to his hands and feet. He coughed from the sudden punch to his left side inflicted by a guard before he and the other guards made their way out.

Moans of desperate men echoed off the walls: men in pain, men in sorrow and hopelessness. Nicholas surveyed the room slowly, taking inventory of the prisoners, but his eyes hadn't yet adjusted to the dark ruins of the room. He squinted. From the coughs, whines, and conversation, he estimated at least fifty men in the few large cells that inhabited the place.

Nicholas lowered his head and closed his eyes as he whispered softly, "Dear Lord…"

Hours had passed. She was in his head and heart. He thought about her soft voice. It almost echoed in his mind loud enough for the other prisoners to hear. He dreamed about her touch, her beautiful eyes and hair, and that soft, precious, intimate, moist kiss they almost shared. His heart longed for her. His Sharon: his rose. She was his soul mate. Could she…

Crack! The whip crossed Nicholas's chest, snapping at his side just below his armpit, splitting his skin and waking him up from his daydream.

"The Emperor wants to see you now," ordered the guard.

Diocletian, the Roman Emperor, slumped sideways in his oversized chair like a bored teenage boy. Two guards walked in with Nicholas sandwiched between them.

"Leave us," he commanded the soldiers. When the door shut behind the guards, he turned to Nicholas and sneered, "So you're the great Saint Nick?"

Nicholas didn't answer.

"It's amazing what a celebrity you've become. If you really are the man of God that they say you are, I'm told that you can heal me? The doctors say I'm dying. But a real God can heal me. So touch me, Saint Nicholas! Do your magic!"

Nicholas responded, "You hunted me down just to pray for you?"

"Maybe. I also wanted to see what this Saint Nick looked like...without the disguise." The Emperor cracked a smile. "Call it curiosity or boredom." He sniffed, scratching his nose absently.

"What about burning down the monasteries? What about the other monks you've imprisoned?" Nicholas persisted, trying to look the Emperor in the eye.

Somehow, the Emperor evaded his gaze, staring at a spot behind the Bishop. "Again, curiosity. Have you ever had an ant bite? That little tiny thing leaves an awful sting. Put a whole colony of ants together and they can take down a cow. Have you ever put an ant in a puddle of water? Eventually he finds his way out...and so you put him in again and again, until...he stops struggling for survival. It's easier to just set the ant on fire...or the colony for that matter." Diocletian picked his teeth and sat forward. "Your Christian friends are nothing but ants that keep biting, annoying my people and my plans. Your theology leads to rebellion and is anti-modernism. I can't build a modern empire if you Christians keep insisting that moving forward is a way of evil. But I'll tell you what... If you can heal me, maybe I'll let you go and think about believing your God is real. If you can't, then I'll know you're nothing more than a fake." He smirked, trying to corner Nicholas with his words.

"It is not right to test the Lord our God. It is God himself who does the healing, not I. He chooses whom he wants to heal," Nicholas spoke in a soft, monotone voice.

"Our God? *Your God!* Pray for me! I'm waiting!"

Diocletian closed his eyes and leaned forward. Nicholas hesitated. He glanced at the stone side table beside the Emperor's chair. His eyes were drawn to the short, silver blade, with an ivory handle, just inches away from him. He slowly moved towards the Emperor. The knife was within his grasp.

He hesitated again. Nicholas slowly lifted his right arm and placed his hand on the Emperor's head. The Emperor's neck was exposed. *I can take him, now,* Nicholas thought. *I can end all this evil, all this persecution of Christians...* He was tempted. His heart raced. His hand was shaking. Perhaps all of his street fighting days as a youth were just training for this very moment! Perhaps God gave him this opportunity!

He quickly dismissed his thoughts, remembering David when he had the opportunity to take King Saul's life. As much as he hated this killer of Christians, this evil man, God was ultimately in control. It was a time to surrender and ultimately trust in God. He felt the Holy Spirit screaming at him, telling him to be the man of God that he was created to be, which meant not killing Diocletian, even if the man was saturated with evil. *Trust in Christ.*

Nicholas began to pray. "Our Father who art in Heaven, by the blood of Jesus, the Christ, which was shed on the cross for our sins, I ask that you would heal this man of his infirmities... And Lord, forgive him of his sins. May he find out who you really are."

The Emperor laughed mockingly, as if he thought Nicholas's prayer was humorous and trite.

Nicholas found his face against the slimy, wet wall of the dungeon once again; just before the Roman guard thrust his knee into the ex-Bishop's back. He pulled Nicholas back again away from the wall and forced him down the steps, steering him to one of the few prison cells filled with a dozen prisoners.

The prison door opened and the guard threw Nicholas onto the floor face first. His head ricocheted off the ground, knocking him out.

"Bishop Nicholas?"

Bishop Bartholomew handed the official papers to Cardinal Michaels. His heart raced with joy as he reiterated what they said.

"The Archbishop said to reinstate Nicholas as a Bishop!"

The Cardinal snatched the papers out of the Bishop's hand and began to read it for himself.

> *Last night the Lord gave me the strangest dream of sorts. The Lord informed me that we are to reinstate Nicholas as Bishop; that our entire faith and the future of our Christianity depend on it. I ask that you join me in dismissal of the action against Bishop Nicholas, and that as Cardinal, you will apply affirmative rehabilitation for the Bishop, upon his reinstatement.*

"Too bad he's not here to be reinstated," the Cardinal said with a devilish smile. "I had a similar dream. But it's too late, isn't it? Besides, his monastery's nothing but ashes by now."

"Why do you hate him so?" demanded a disappointed Bishop Bartholomew. "What are you afraid of?"

The Cardinal, stunned by the remark of the Bishop, took a deep breath, turned around and spoke slowly. "I did what I could to protect *your* monastery."

"You can make a deal with the devil, but that doesn't mean the devil's going to keep his end of the bargain," the Bishop timidly answered back.

I'm free, he thought to himself. The prison walls contained him, but his heart was as wild and free as a teenage boy. And he was in love.

His dreams turned to her once again. Nicholas remembered Sharon's dimple positioned on her left cheek that grew deeper as she smiled. He remembered her pearl-like teeth. Ah, and her lips. They glistened a ruby red contrasted by her white furry clothes and the scarf around her slender neck. He faced low temperatures he never knew existed while in those mountains, but was inwardly warmed by her companionship.

"I'm free," he said out loud to himself again. He was no longer bound to the slavery of his position. His religion had no hold on him. He was as free as any man in a free world. He could marry. He could love and get loved back. He could give into his passions. He wondered about the physical intimacy his mind always forbade. Nothing could stop him from loving his sweetheart, the tender, redheaded Sharon. Nothing could get in their way. Not man, not God...*okay, maybe God*, he thought to himself, but certainly not Cardinal St. Michaels or the monastery. Love was his for the taking, and taking Sharon as his bride was his passionate dream.

He loved children. He thought about the many times he'd watch a family and wonder what it felt like; to be a part of something physically greater, something two passionate soul mates created by their love, something miniature that physically resembled the combination of their union. He wondered what it felt like to hold such a tiny being and to raise it as his own. Perhaps he would one day find out.

"Bishop Nicholas!" The voice echoed in his ear.

The numbness of his face began to wear off and the pain became very real, real enough to moan.

"Bishop Nicholas!" the voice rang out once again.

His eyes slowly pried themselves open to see a monk sitting beside him. The brother had part of his scalp missing. A long, fresh scar stretched from the left side of the man's forehead, down to his eyebrow. Patches of hair covered the man's chin, face, and neck. Nicholas didn't recognize him.

"Bishop Nicholas, it's me! David!"

Nicholas sat up as quickly as he could and hugged him. "I've been praying for you!"

"As we have for you!" said the young monk.

Nicholas kissed him affectionately on the forehead, like a father to his son. "Have you been here all this time?"

"Yes, some of the Christians have been here for months. Others who spoke out boldly were eventually hung. There are new arrivals daily, from all over Asia Minor. The Emperor put a bounty on your head, offering lenience to anyone who'd bring you to him."

"Are all the prisoners here brothers?" asked Nicholas.

"For the most part. They released a number of criminals just to make room for us. Besides, we were getting the criminals saved. They figured we'd do more damage by preaching to them," he chortled.

Growing serious, David quickly glanced around the room. "What do we do now?" he questioned the man he admired.

"What do you think we do? We pray! Nothing's too big for our Lord. Remember that, brother. He is the Master of miracles."

"Then it is a miracle we must pray for. Unless Diocletian dies soon, we're all pretty much dead men."

"And we'll feast together in the kingdom of Heaven. Do not fear, brother."

The three-century-old dungeon was placed underground, with no trace or entrance to the outside world above, except by a wooden horizontal door on chains located at the top of the stairs. The staircase was usually heavily guarded by the most evil of soldiers. It was often a post or duty place of probation for soldiers who became too violent with citizens and needed to be rehabilitated. And several of the guards were just deformed figures that the Emperor felt were too "ugly" to represent a Roman soldier in daylight.

The entire prison could hear and feel the sounds of the chains pulling the trap door open every time a prisoner was brought in, or when a prisoner was leaving for his final verdict. It was a bittersweet sound. During daytime it meant a few seconds of witnessing natural light, a sight hungered by all the prisoners, but the clanks of the chains also brought the nauseating stench of death for fellow believers and those without status in the community.

David's stomach knotted as the chains clanked against the metal loops that held them in place once again, allowing the flat door to rise. There was quite a commotion on the other side.

Another bloodied and beaten victim began the descent. The soldiers steered the broken, black haired man in red down the staircase. His hair was a mess, soot covered his face, and his clothes were torn and burned near the bottom half of his robe. Despair masked him. He gaped forward, seeing past anything physical, reflecting the hopelessness in his soul. He was defeated.

Two beefy soldiers directed him to a lonely cell on the other side of the prison, about twenty-five or so yards from David and Nicholas.

David questioned, "Isn't that Cardinal Michaels?"

"I think so," Nicholas hesitantly spoke.

"Cardinal Michaels! Cardinal Michaels!" David whisper-yelled.

The Cardinal remained in a trance, staring forward, motionless, unaware that anyone was trying to get his attention, and still trying to figure out how he ended up there.

Nana and Papa finally arrived for the Christmas Eve meal. My wife called from the kitchen, "It's time to eat! Girls, you need to wash up!" Makayla rushed to the bathroom, obsessed with the bubbles from the soap dispenser.

Gabriella slowly climbed down from my lap. "This is a yucky story, Daddy."

I glanced at the boys who were more than intrigued by now. I could tell by their faces that they had gained a new respect for the jolly old man in red.

Chapter 12

Dinner was wonderful. I was stuffed with turkey and gravy (our family tradition), cranberry sauce, rolls, green beans, some kind of funky cornbread casserole, sweet potatoes with marshmallows on top, and of course, cherry pie for dessert. My mother and father brought the casserole and sweet potatoes, and my sister brought the dessert. Thankfully, my wife made the turkey this year. It was mouthwatering. Each tender bite literally melted in your mouth.

The only red on the table was the beautiful tablecloth designed with off-red satin paisleys, unlike other years. Before my grandmother's ill health, our Christmas Eve celebrations were held at her house. She always feared undercooking the turkey, the result being a table full of guests swigging tea every five seconds to get the dry meat down. I likened it to swallowing sand. Even the gravy wasn't moist enough to help.

I was seven years old when Uncle Barry attempted to go to Grandmother's fridge during dinner and pull out the ketchup bottle. Needless to say, Grandmother was highly offended and almost stopped him, mid-step. However, he pulled out the "I'm Jewish" card. "I put ketchup on everything!" he explained.

Being a Christian family, we knew nothing about Jewish culture, or if he was making it up. I think I was the first to say, "Let me try it!" Before my mother could grab the ketchup bottle out of my hands, it poured in thick clumps all over my turkey. It worked. Thicker than gravy, the wet, red substance diluted the dry sand enough to get it down my esophagus. By the end of the meal, almost every family member under the age of thirty had ketchup on his or her turkey. This became an annual tradition, until, of course, my wife took over the cooking.

We made normal small talk, and the traditional family stories resurfaced, as I assumed they would, of my Dad nailing the Christmas tree to the floor, and me biting off the glass ear of the gingerbread man. Elisha followed in my footsteps this year as she bit the arm off a spree ornament, thinking it was a cookie. Luckily, between the two of us, my sister and I had six kids, never wasting a moment to create new stories to add for the following year's annual meal.

I retired to the living room once again, and the boys all followed. The girls made their way to the bedroom to play with Barbie dolls, the moms worked in the kitchen, and Dad sat in his old favorite chair next to me, with Jackson climbing up into his lap.

"Finish your story, Uncle Matt!" Jackson begged.

With the girls gone, I figured this would be a perfect time to include the gruesome details of their holiday hero. I propped back in my chair, sighed, squinted, and continued my tale.

…The valiant warrior sliced his way through any flesh that got in his way. His sword had slain hundreds, if not thousands. His army was unstoppable. But he was cornered. With no pagan god of his in sight, he turned to the God of his mother and called out, "What do I do?"

For the first time in history, this victor was about to call his army to retreat—to return to the hills and scatter. He was tired, and his soldiers were more tired. The sound of fear and abandon, a ram's horn was about to blow, when suddenly, there it happened.

He couldn't believe it, had he not seen it himself. A giant crucifix glowed in front of him. *Was it imaginary? Was it real?* He wondered, as he squinted at it. The glowing cross became engulfed by flames and then burned itself away.

He remembered his mother, often clenching the cross she held so dear as she prayed for his safety. This was the God of his mother, the God who hung himself on a cross for the salvation of others, the God of the people his close friend and Emperor, Diocletian, was persecuting.

The warrior regained his strength, and his mother's God gave him motivation. His army pressed on and penetrated the enemy until every boundary belonged to him, every city was captured, and every leader surrendered or was slain.

Morning came, but the prisoners had no way of knowing it, except by the opening and closing of the trap door. If it was dark outside with no light, then it was either night or early morning. The next time the door was lifted, if light came through, then it was assumed that a new day had come. However, this calendar method wasn't foolproof as sometimes the sun didn't shine or the door would remain shut for days.

The newer prisoners could still tell time by their stomach pangs, and several of them grumbled about their morning hunger.

Dong! Dong! Dong!

David sat up quickly from his slumber. Another monk stared back at him and gulped.

"That's the bell of death," said David to Nicholas. "Every time they ring it, another prisoner is hung." He rubbed his wounds absently.

The other monk said aloud, "Three rings... Three hangin's!"

The chains slowly began grinding through the loops again as the door was lifted and the morning light cast her face on the gloomy stairs. Two Roman soldiers made their way down to the dungeon and stopped at Nicholas's cage.

They inventoried the men inside and then made their way to the connecting cage.

The soldiers grabbed a hairy, thin man who had a beard that resembled a lion's mane.

He fought and pleaded, "No! No!" exposing his broken teeth and infected gums.

The soldiers dragged and pushed him to the stairs and beat him a few times into submission, finally dragging him out of the dismal pit to his final destination.

David swallowed. "You never know when they're coming for you."

"No last rights or anything!" another monk fretted aloud.

Nicholas responded, "The good Lord won't let us go before our time."

"Yeah, that's what I'm afraid of! What if it's my time?" questioned a nervous David.

The prisoners became silent again as the footsteps echoed down the corridor and grew louder with each cadence.

One of the soldiers made his way to Nicholas's and David's cell, eyeing the prisoners like a shopper in a meat market, deciding what meat to buy. "You!" he demanded, as he pointed at David. "Come with me!"

"It's time!" said David, sarcastically, taking a deep breath and gulping the sour air. The words barely escaped his throat.

Nicholas watched as David ascended the stairs into the light and out of sight. He said a quick prayer for the monk. It wasn't all that bad, Nicholas thought. It was almost symbolic. What an honor to die for the sake of our Lord Jesus Christ! What a life truly lived! Pretty soon David would be ascending another case of stairs into the light he thought...*the TRUE light.*

It's why every Christian truly lives. It's why every monk becomes a monk. It's always been about the afterlife, about spending an eternity with Jesus, the King of kings and Lord of lords. It's about knowing the God of the universe, the creator of all mankind, and living with him eternally in a place without sin, a place without pain, hurt, death, greed, or sorrow. And David was about to see it all firsthand.

Diminutive Andy and Harry made their way down the snowy peaks and through the thick of the forest, trying to bypass the towns or people who might recognize them. Two reindeer pulled their sled, and a satin green sack of wooden toys and candies filled the back. They were hoping to show Nicholas their beginnings of a prosperous operation, delivering the first of many bags of goodies to come.

Several of the monks inched their way around Nicholas. Even in such a dark place, he was a glowing pillar of strength with words and prayers of encouragement. They were drawn to him.

Singing praises to the Lord, Nicholas and the lonely monk prisoners were quickly silenced by the opening of the trap door above the stairs again. Marcus found himself the newest detainee, shoved down the stairs and into the cell next to his mentor.

"Marcus!"

Marcus quickly scurried his way through the grimy mud floor and weeds over to the edge of the cell facing Nicholas. His bruised face and buggy eyes told the story of his recent occurrence with Roman soldiers.

The Roman army made their presence known through all of Asia Minor, conquering anyone and anything that challenged them. One man alone was responsible for this endeavor to take over every city within reach, a man of bravery and strength, a man not afraid, but to be feared, a man so powerful that the only person he answered to was Diocletian himself.

Constantine proudly carried the heads of his enemies' leaders in burlap bags, strapped around his saddle, on his ride back to Byzantium to win the praise of his Emperor, Diocletian. Their dark crimson blood formulated a jelly-like oozing substance at the bottom of the bags, leaving stains down his beautiful white Stallion, the exotic and perfectly toned creature adorned with the blood and scars of battle like a fierce warrior himself.

Upon entering the city gates, the two marched a victory gallop in confidence, proudly displaying the detached heads as trophies. Citizens stared in fear, while children eyed the bags with curiosity. His army closely followed, his men trying to mimic his valiance, but unsuccessfully doing so.

"Water for the horse!" Constantine commanded the privates as he dismounted.

"There is a man named Constantine...," Nicholas started.

Marcus interrupted, "I know this man. He's a very dangerous man. He's killed more men than any man in history. Even his horse knows how to kill people they say."

"He's God's chosen vessel. The Lord has put him on my heart. We must pray for him. He's our only hope. Trust in God," replied Nicholas.

"Pray for what? That he doesn't kill us?"

"That, too. Pray that he finds the Lord, and that God softens his heart and he gives his life and this nation over to him. Get all the monks to pray. God will move. I promise."

The two midgets found themselves at the Myra monastery, frantically searching for their saint, surveying the damage and looking for a promise: a promise that Nicholas was still alive. His beloved Sharon was victim to her illness once again. In desperation, the midgets made a dangerous quest from the mountains, hoping and praying that Nicholas would return to bring healing a second time.

They were oblivious to the conquered town or their hero's capture.

Harry looked back at the green sack of toys. "So what now?"

"Well, we need to find out where he is. They probably took him to Byzantium."

"What about the toys?"

"Let's find a place to stash it! I still say we deliver them all by time of the festival, with or without the Bishop."

"What about Sharon?" reminded Harry, frowning.

"If we don't find Nicholas to pray for her, I don't think it matters if we come back or not."

Diocletian showered Constantine with praise, a parade, and gifts of gold, fine materials, and rarities. Constantine proudly took his place on the right side of his mentor, savoring the ego lifts as Diocletian bragged on him in front of the people. His words of affirmation to his young successor were mingled with jealousy and fear, spoken through clinched teeth.

What would be next for the world's greatest conqueror? Neither of them talked about it, but they both knew that the Emperor's time was short. Nicholas's attempts at healing were futile. The Emperor's coughs had worsened, and blood frequently found its way from his lungs.

It was hard for Constantine to watch his friend dying, but even harder to watch his mother dying. She was plagued with the same illness. All of his conquering could do nothing to save her, and he felt helpless. He often turned to his pagan gods and offered sacrifices for her healing, and for his Emperor, against Mom's approval.

The petite grey haired woman with rough, aged skin knelt at the side of her bed. Although she was too sick to be out of bed, her allegiance to her God gave her the strength to do so. "Dear heavenly Father, I pray that the saints are released in Jesus' name. I pray that you would remove Diocletian from power, and that my son would serve you, follow you, and do the right thing. May he know the Lord Jesus I serve…"

She fell asleep lying half in and half out of bed. She was fatigued, too tired to even finish her thoughts or prayers. As her mind drifted, she had a vision. A tall, thin glowing man with fading hair walked up to her in the room and placed his hand on her.

Then he spoke. "The Lord has heard your prayers." She felt a surge of energy jolt her body. She looked up to see that the man had vanished.

His beloved Sharon was in his dreams again, but this time his deep sleep led him to a nightmare. The skies around her were grey, and as they talked, pink flowers were falling to the ground, wilting and fading to a dark blue, then purple, then black. The vision of her face was fading as she kept coughing. The man of God understood the frightful dream and began praying for her, even in his sleep.

Clank!

Nicholas awoke to his cell creaking open. Two prison guards grabbed him and lifted him up, dragging him through the murky corridor, up the stairs, and through the dimly lit opening.

The sun hid her face behind a series of grey clouds, yet it was still too bright for Nicholas to open his eyes. He squinted at his surroundings as the guards continued to drag him past the town and into the backside of the stone and marble arena. His feet were cut from the dungeon, being dragged up the stairs, and onto the rocky road. Now, the crimson blood painted each step he took on the beautiful stone platform, leading to the stage.

Nicholas gazed through sleep-deprived eyes at the awesome structure. Hundreds of rows of stone seats were before him, organized in a semi-circle, and layered upon one another until their end about ten stories high. Large smoothed semi-circle archways stood at the top of the arena, with stone masks chiseled into the walls. The structure was definitely Roman, a surmising symbol of Rome's presence in the new world.

The soldiers strapped Nicholas to a wooden structure using leather cords. Then they left him alone in the barren, open-aired theatre. He watched, still squinting, as several buzzards flew overhead in the amber sky. He couldn't decide which hurt worse: the open wounds on his feet or the penetrating, ice-cold winds blowing through his ragged clothes.

Hours had passed and other prisoners were brought out to the platform, none of which Nicholas recognized. They were strapped to the wooden structure adjacent to

Nicholas. It was obvious that he was the main attraction. By now, his lips were tinted blue from the cold.

By midday, the emaciated Nicholas had weakened in the blistering wind and partial sun, too weak to notice the hundreds of spectators that had accumulated in the bench-like stone and marble seats, spread out on all levels like fans waiting for a sporting event.

Within an hour the crowd had thickened and Nicholas glanced to his left, noticing that the empty chairs on the stage were now filled with Rome's finest. Diocletian sat in the middle seat, a grand seat meshed with red velvet and a raised back. Next to him was a woman of stature. She was dressed in fine jewels, a light blue dress, and her hair was done in braids. On her other side was the warrior, leader of Rome's army, the crowd pleaser and enforcer, Constantine the Great.

Nicholas stared at them through half-opened eyes, in and out of consciousness, not even noticing the soldiers to his other side or in front of him.

Whack!

The young soldier slapped the whip across Nicholas's chest. Nicholas looked at the soldier with eyes of love. His face was soft, his heart and spirit broken. The soldier looked intently at Nicholas, trying desperately not to lose his composure. There was something about Nicholas's presence. The soldier could sense it. Nicholas continued to stare, love penetrating, permeating the thick air between the two.

Whack!

The undeveloped soldier forced an angry stare at Nicholas. The broken man of God kept smiling back, his large eyes pulling the soldier in. Perhaps it was the lack of sleep, perhaps it was the lack of nutrition, perhaps it was the spirit of God, and perhaps it was *real*. Whatever it was, Nicholas saw a boy from the orphanage in the eyes of the young man before him. He loved the young soldier.

Whack!

The soldier couldn't stop staring back.

For a moment, all was forgotten. The sounds of the spectators, the commanding rule of the leaders, and the cries of the prisoners were all silenced in the minds of Nicholas and the young man.

The boy had broken. He was, in fact, a boy. He'd enlisted in the army to prove his manhood. But at this moment, reality set in, compassion had won, and the young boy inside returned to the surface and encompassed this wanna-be man in military dress.

At Diocletian's consent, the young soldier cut the straps on Nicholas's arms to set him free from his wooden and leather captor. Nicholas had no strength as he fell to the boy soldier, wrapping his arms around him like a father, forcing the boy to hold him up. Tears streamed down the soldier's face, wiping them on Nicholas's shoulder, trying to regain his composure in front of his commander. Two soldiers rushed up and took Nicholas by the arms and hurried him over to Diocletian, but still in center stage as to present him to the crowd.

Diocletian loved the spotlight, whether good or bad. He knew that making a sport of his sentencing would give him the exposure and favor he preferred. He was building a name for himself, desiring to leave a legacy once he was gone.

Nicholas glanced to the left at the warrior Constantine long enough to see beyond the curiosity in his eyes. He thought about the many prayers he and the monks lifted for the great warrior and future Emperor, wondering if God had heard them.

Constantine looked at the young soldier, still motionless, crumbled to his knees in front of the wooden rod that once held Nicholas. Another soldier came up behind the young man, aggressively preparing to take him away. "Leave him!" Constantine yelled, seeing a glimpse of his own history in the young soldier. The older soldier stepped away.

Diocletian addressed the crowd. "You see before you a mere man who some claim is a saint, a healer! But I've put him to the test, and he's no healer. He's a fraud!"

The crowd roared both their approvals and disapprovals.

"This man and his friends destroyed the temple of Artemis!" Diocletian yelled in anger, waiting for the rage of the crowd.

He turned to the battered Nicholas. "You are charged with treason, promoting a false religion, speaking against the gods of Rome, destroying the temple of Artemis, leading people into rebellion, hindering modernism, and trying to avoid the Roman tax."

The crowd howled.

"For your crimes..." Diocletian smiled, holding back the verdict a few seconds to create suspense as if he were putting on a show for the spectators. "You...will...be... PUT TO DEATH!"

The people in the stands were uncontrollable at this point; some were in tears, others were enraged. Midgets Andy and Harry remained stricken and motionless as they observed from the side of the theatre, hidden from the crowd.

Constantine watched, wavering, as the soldiers took turns whipping Nicholas—one lash for every offense. "Enough!" the warrior cried out to his men. The soldiers stopped the lashes, took Nicholas by the arms and dragged him off the stage and out of sight.

Gabriella and Makayla worked their way back into the living room, Christmas-dressed Barbies in hand. They remembered the story being told and quieted the imaginary voices of their dolls. Makayla climbed into my lap, and Gabriella followed, not wanting her sister to get attention or affection without an equal share of her own.

Chapter 13

Nicholas took his last deep breath of fresh air before being forced down the stairs to the underground prison and thrust into the lonely cell with Cardinal Michaels.

The man of God sat motionless. For once, he appreciated the warmth of the cell. It wasn't really warm at all, but he was protected from the blustery weather. He rested his head against the wall and took shallow breaths, his eyes heavy. It appeared the Cardinal was staring at the blood crusted on the Bishop's feet.

"I take it you were sentenced to die, too?" Nicholas quietly asked the Cardinal. He waited for a response, but the Cardinal appeared to be void of reality, lacking in conversation, and continued to stare at a crack along the far wall.

The burns on the Cardinal's legs caught the Bishop's attention. He reached down to lift the Cardinal's cloak to get a better look. The Cardinal responded automatically by pushing Nicholas's hands away, still not saying a word. He looked into the Cardinal's eyes and the Cardinal responded with eyes of fear and loneliness, like a scared child, shaking with horror. Nicholas gently attempted to lift the Cardinal's cloak again, this time successfully exposing the deep burn and mangled flesh crusted with dry blood on the Cardinal's calves.

"Dear God…" Nicholas spoke in revulsion. He placed his hands directly on the burnt flesh and began to pray.

The all-too familiar sound of metal chains and loops clanking echoed the halls once again. The prisoners all watched to see who it could be at this time of the day.

Constantine made his way down the stairs and into the prison, holding a rag over his face and nose to avoid the penetrating stench. He and a guard walked to the first cell where Marcus was held and the guard placed his key in it. The door was jammed.

"He's over here!" another soldier yelled out to his superior.

The guard took his key from the slot and made his way over to Nicholas's cell. "Come with me!" he directed Nicholas, as the prison guard opened death row's cell door. All of the prisoners from their cages watched frightfully.

Sluggishly, Nicholas followed Constantine, sandwiched between two soldiers. They found a little room just above the prison that appeared to be some sort of resting place for the guards.

"Leave us!" the leader told his men puppets.

His men walked out, closing the door behind them.

"I'm caught in a bind. Do you know who I am?"

"Yes… Constantine."

Constantine paced the floor. "My mother is ill. She's dying. She shares your beliefs…your religion. I'm told you can save her."

"The Lord can heal her," Nicholas corrected him softly.

"I can't bring her here because she's too ill, and I can't take you to her because I'd be charged with treason." He continued to pace for a moment.

Nicholas tore off a piece of his sleeve and silently prayed over it, rubbing it firmly between his fingers. "Give this to her."

Constantine took the torn cloth from Nicholas and nodded. He took a deep breath and walked away, then turned around again.

"Listen…when I was in battle, I heard a voice. I saw a vision of a large, glowing cross. Do you think I'm crazy?"

"God created you for such a time as this, Constantine. He has his hand on your life, but you need to give it to him—to Christ."

"Humph!" Constantine responded, almost humored by Nicholas. Here he was, Constantine the great. His life was perfect. He was feared by many and adored by his own people. What would it mean to *give his life* to Christ? What would it cost him? "Guard!" Constantine yelled, turning to the door and exiting the room.

A large Roman guard entered the room and took a hold of Nicholas, forcing him, without resistance, to the underground chambers.

The guard fumbled with the lock to the cell that detained Marcus and the other prisoners. He finally pried the malfunctioned mechanism open and threw Nicholas inside, either forgetting that he came from death row, or secretly following the orders of his commander. He closed the gate, which made an unfamiliar connecting sound, but not thinking of it, the soldier walked away and out of the dungeon.

As the prisoners watched the last guard make his exit, and the door above the stairs close for a final time, they finagled the lock of their cell to release, setting all the men free. One by one the prisoners forced themselves out of the steel bars and down the corridor to the stairs of freedom. One of the prisoners grabbed the small lighted torch that was attached to the wall.

Marcus tugged at Nicholas's hand. "C'mon! Now's our chance! We can be free!"

"Marcus… No." Nicholas gave a disapproving nod, keeping his place on the ground behind the bars.

Marcus let go, looking at his mentor with frightful eyes, this time disobedient to his orders as he turned around and followed the other prisoners up the flight of stairs.

The prisoners forced the door open. Nicholas and the Cardinal couldn't see anything, but they heard the horror of each prisoner sharing the same fate of a Roman sword. One by one they heard the screams until everything was silent.

Moments later, a rush of heavy footsteps descended the stairs as several soldiers came to investigate the remaining prisoners.

A breathless soldier ran to the open gate carrying the torch, glanced at the lock, and noticed Nicholas still inside the open cell. The soldier quickly picked up the Bishop, dragged him across the muddy floor, and shoved him back into the cage with the Cardinal, slamming the prison door behind him.

Nicholas looked to the Cardinal who was almost in the fetal position, his thumb to his lip as if he wanted to suck it. His eyes were still vacant, reflecting that he was in a far away land mentally. Nicholas quickly glanced to his leg again. The Cardinal felt him watching and pulled his legs closer to his body.

"Praise God," Nicholas mumbled under his breath, noticing that the Cardinal's leg was now completely different— no burns, dried blood, or deformities. The Lord had healed him.

The first hard snow of the season was falling. Had they not been underground, the prisoners would have all frozen to death. Nicholas tended the little tree struggling to grow in the bitter, dark cell. Miraculously, this tree defied all odds. Born within the prison cell soil, it managed to get enough light to somehow stay alive, however puny it was.

The Cardinal watched Nicholas day by day, still not saying a word, but obvious by his body language and facial expressions about his disapproval of Nicholas's green thumb project. Enough was enough, and the Cardinal finally gained the courage to say a few words.

"Why are you wasting your time?" the Cardinal gargled with a deep, throaty voice.

Nicholas smiled at the Cardinal, happy that he finally spoke.

The two paused and turned their attention to the bells of death ringing outside. They'd become so used to them that fear no longer seized them. After the last bell rang, the Cardinal turned his attention back to Nicholas. "It's going to die, just like you and me. Besides, it's a fir. It won't grow any fruit for you to eat, so, if that was your plan..."

"No," responded Nicholas, "It's a symbol of hope. If this plant can survive in here, then we can too. It's not food; just hope."

The Cardinal shrugged and snickered. His eyes were worn and weary, his body slumped almost horizontal against the prison cell wall. He finally appeared *with it*, regardless of how exhausted he looked.

Clank! Clank! Clank!

The prison door opened and two unfamiliar guards made their way slowly down the steps, down the corridor and to the entrance of their cell. One of the guards waved his torch in front of the two men of the cloth, while the other surveyed the remaining prisoners.

Fear seized the Cardinal as he looked at Nicholas, who returned the look like a boy caught stealing candy in a candy store.

The oversized, rugged soldier placed the key in the door and turned it, then, forced the prison cell door open.

The Cardinal's legs squirmed, pushing him up against the wall where he was sitting. His breath escaped him as the two soldiers grabbed him by the arms and pulled him out of the cage and into the corridor.

He finally gained his breath, wrestling with death, but easily losing as he was dragged down the hallway. The Cardinal yelled out, "I'm sorry! I'm sorry!" He looked at Nicholas, his eyes soft and filled with sorrow, "I'm sorry, Bishop, please forgive me!"

The soldiers dragged him out of sight, but Nicholas could still hear the horrid echoes of his screams, "Forgive meeeeeee!!!!" The Cardinal's shadow slowly diminished on the walls of the hallway as they proceeded.

"The Lord forgives you, and so do I," Nicholas mumbled under his breath, returning to his tree and reshaping the ground around it.

He continued his daily prayers, lifting up Constantine and his mother, God's transformation in Asia Minor, salvation for the lost, for the dwarfs, the missing orphans, and for his beloved Sharon.

His thoughts of her were the only thing keeping him warm these bitterly cold days. He thought about how chilly it must be in the mountains this time of year, and wondered if...and then he wondered if he should even be wondering thoughts such as these...if she would want them to live in the mountains with the dwarfs, or in his home town of Myra. He didn't care. He just needed one thing to be happy he thought: Sharon.

He thought about his calling, wondering if his expulsion from the church as Bishop was truly a gift of God in disguise.

"A family," he said quietly to himself. "Am I too old for a family?" He marveled at the idea. He had never wanted one before. Suffering the death of both of his parents at an early age persuaded him to never marry, because marriage meant children, and children meant family. He couldn't bear the thought of possibly causing the pain to one of his children that he dealt with as a child, if he were to have any.

The orphans at the monastery's orphanage became his family. They were his children, and he loved each and every one of them sincerely. He knew where they were and where they'd been in life. He had been there. However, his acceptance by the other orphans wasn't always so.

He was always the outsider in his youth. He was considered eccentric and odd. The other boys often teased him and harassed him, calling him sissy, pretty boy, freak, and other not-so-nice names. He would often find himself punching or fighting the other children for his own protection, and weekly brawls with bullies taught him a thing or two about defending himself. It wasn't that he couldn't pulverize every adolescent who ever made fun of him. It's just that he felt guilty doing it, and the tender hearted young Nicholas would always cry after hurting the other child, even if he didn't start it. It was easier to run away or put up with the abuse than to go through the strong emotions of remorse every time he punched a kid or hurt someone.

God became his friend; his only friend. While others were playing games, he would find a tree and rest beneath it, pouring his heart out to his Maker. He'd watch the other boys at play and often ask, "God, why did you make me like this?" He felt like a leper. God gave Nicholas an immense amount of sensitivity and compassion, much more than most young men. He was a nurturer. Even as a child, he always watched out for the littler ones at the orphanage, making sure they were well-fed, properly cleaned, and emotionally secure. He would befriend the new orphans, and often held the younger ones, as they would cry for their abandoning or deceased parents at night. The older males would tease him and call him "mom."

"Who would want to marry me?" a young Nicholas often asked himself. Girls wanted the warrior, hero, or stud that could kill game with his bare hands. The nurturer seemed to have nothing to offer. He loved children, animals, education, and cooking—things that a female would normally love. He had a heart for the oppressed. He was compassionate and giving, yet he thought he had nothing to give the opposite sex. He wasn't their *type*.

But he was in love. He was in love with Jesus, and he wasn't afraid to say it. Over the years, underneath the pines, he would talk to his Savior and best friend, and he would get to know him more and more intimately. His heightened sensitivity and time spent with his Savior taught him how to hear God's voice or sense his leading, and time and time again God would prove that he heard Nicholas too.

When he first joined the monastery as a monk, he talked about his Jesus like a person who truly knew the Savior on a personal level, someone who had truly experienced a life with him. The other monks considered him peculiar and a borderline nutcase. They were formal and religious, they knew Scripture and protocol, but very few seemed to know the same Jesus that Nicholas appeared to know.

"You talk about Jesus as if he's your girlfriend," the other monks would tease, just like the boys in the orphanage from his childhood. Teasing became a way of life towards someone so eccentric, unusual, and unconventional.

Peter was the first monk who befriended Nicholas in the monastery. He, too, didn't know Jesus the way Nicholas did, but Nicholas's talks of a personal God who wanted intimacy with his creation was the inspiration that pulled Peter in. His thirst for a deeper connection with God drew him to Nicholas, and the two boys became the best of friends.

Nicholas often thought about Peter and wondered what happened to him. He said a number of prayers for him, for his safety, and for God's blessings in his life. He wondered if Peter already found his way to Heaven, basking in God's heavenly glory in Paradise. Nicholas grasped the cage with his hands and Peter felt close, too close. In his heart, Nicholas felt as if Peter had been there previously, touching the very same bars.

He remembered his prayers again as a lonely fourteen year old. He would be at the prayer tree, sitting beneath her branches, crying, begging God for a best friend. He longed for a connection that other males had. He sometimes blamed his Dad for not being there, wondering if he would be *normal* if he had a father to raise him. But then he'd remember that the other orphans were fatherless too. He just didn't have the testosterone levels they had, and for some reason this abnormality hindered him from male bonding.

The Bishop who resided at Myra during his youth always encouraged the young man, "Nicholas, God made you special. He doesn't make mistakes."

It was this very same Bishop that continually spoke words of affirmation to a hurting teenage boy, taking him under his wing and inspiring the young man to follow in his footsteps as a man of the cloth.

"The prayer tree..." Nicholas said out loud in remembrance, calm and smiling, looking down at the new tree he was trying to birth. He was so deep in thought that he didn't even realize the gate opening and the soldiers descending the stairs and coming to his door.

Chapter 14

The bells of death echoed in the city streets, calling the curious and bored. Before noon the coliseum was completely packed, much more than the last time Nicholas was there. It appeared that everyone in Byzantium and many cities beyond were present.

Nicholas surveyed the crowd and stage. Diocletian and the pretty woman dressed in blue were missing. Sitting in her seat was a grey haired woman, holding a tissue and staring at Nicholas as if she knew him. Her eyes were wide, waterlogged, and engaging. Her hand trembled as she touched the tissue to her nose, fighting back her tears. Her son approached the seats with several Roman soldiers surrounding him. He sat in Diocletian's seat and placed his hand on his mother, the woman beside him, giving her a reassuring look.

Nicholas looked to the other side of the stage where several ropes formed into nooses hung from a wooden beam. *My entry to Heaven*, Nicholas thought to himself.

Several rookie soldiers brought out six men Nicholas noticed—men who were once powerful forces of the Roman military, militants who hunted after him, Marcus, and Stu. The young soldiers forced the heads of these scandalous men into the life-taking loops that awaited them, preparing them to meet their Maker with the signal of their commander. Nicholas wondered why he was still in chains and not part of the crew to be hung. Perhaps it wasn't his time, as David put it.

Constantine rose from Diocletian's seat, his new throne, to address the crowd. The audience hushed and the man of valor bowed as if he was presenting a play.

"Fine people of Byzantium, and guests from nearby cities, you are all welcome to be here today, this glorious day! Today marks a new day, a new era of time, and you are all witnesses of the things to come. As many of you know, Diocletian is gone, and I, Constantine, a servant of the people, am your new Emperor!"

Constantine waited for the crowd's approval. A soldier yelled, leading the others in applause. Constantine bowed and then lifted his hands to hush the crowd.

"In honor, to celebrate my plans for a new Byzantium (new Rome) and a new Asia Minor, no longer under the threat of fear, but a land belonging to the people, I give to you these six hangings today!"

The crowd cheered as Constantine pointed to the six men dressed in their undergarments, noosed and prepared for death. The ex-soldiers didn't appear so tough or as arrogant as they did the last time Nicholas saw them.

"These six men are a representation of the old days of Byzantium, running a nation in fear and intimidation, persecuting innocent men, discounting men for free thinking! But today, my friends, we bury the old way of life along with these ex-soldiers, these savage murderers, who enforced such evil practices!"

The people roared with satisfaction. Constantine marveled at what he heard. Never in Diocletian's days had the crowds been so responsive, the retired warrior thought to himself.

Taking from his evil mentor and his ideas of making a show out of his life-snuffing, crowd teasing, spectacle treats, Constantine added the extra audible touch of a drum role to his display of hangings—cueing the soldier responsible for removing the firm foundation beneath the feet of the future dead. The crowd gasped as each ex-soldier was hung, one by one, faces turning blue until the neck and head lay limp. After the last ex-soldier stopped struggling and accepted his fate, Constantine lifted his hands to signal the audience into applause. He didn't quite gain the response he thought he would, but that was okay. His next move was sure to be a crowd pleaser, he considered.

The soldier unlocked the chains around Nicholas's wrists and walked him across the platform. As the Bishop got closer to the center, he could see that the old, grey-haired woman sitting next to Constantine wasn't holding a tissue at all. She was, in fact, holding the cloth he gave Constantine. *This must be his mother*, he contemplated.

The woman quivered, recognizing Nicholas as the man in her dreams who prayed for her.

Constantine approached center stage, meeting up with Nicholas. "This man has been condemned to death on false charges!" he yelled to the audience.

The crowd rustled.

"Standing before me is a man that many of us have heard rumors about over the years. Nicholas the Healer! I stand before you and tell you that this man, the Bishop of Myra, is in fact a healer. I am a witness, firsthand, of the miraculous things his God can do through him."

The people hushed.

Constantine addressed Nicholas and the crowd. "I hereby dismiss all charges against you, and restore you as Bishop under Rome's new authority, never to be challenged or questioned again for your faith. And after much investigation and prayerful counsel, I also declare Byzantium and all of Asia Minor a free Christian Empire!" He waited for the applause of the people. "Furthermore, I hereby declare you Saint, by Roman decree!"

Nicholas leaned in and whispered to Constantine, "I don't think that's your decision to make."

Constantine kept his smile, waving at the crowd as they cheered, speaking to Nicholas softly through his teeth, "I'm the Emperor of Rome! I can do whatever I want." Grabbing Nicholas by the hand, the Emperor raised it and pointed to it with his other hand. The people shouted all the more. "I invite you, Saint Nicholas, to join me in

Byzantium, and to be the personal Bishop of this fine city, and to its Emperor, Constantine."

The Emperor grinned, nodding his head at his audience. Then, he stepped back, slightly bowing to Nicholas. The stadium cheered with a volume level that had never been heard in its history.

"Saint Nicholas! Saint Nicholas! Saint Nicholas! Saint Nicholas!" they roared.

The chanting refused to cease, and Nicholas breathed it in, looking around in amazement and awe. The chant was so thick and loud that their words began to run together...

"Saint Nicholas! Saint Nichlas! Sant Nichlas! Santa Claus! Santa Claus! Santa Claus! Santa Claus!"

Being imprisoned, hungry, beaten, frozen, and sleep-deprived can mess with a person's mind. Nicholas thought about this as he humored himself with the question: *"Are they saying Saint Nicholas, or Santa Claus? Who's Santa Claus?"* His head was spinning. He chuckled.

"Daddy, you're silly," Gabriella interrupted.
I paused, looked down at her and responded, "What? You don't think that really happened?"

She giggled, "No!" She laughed so hard her adorable little five year old teeth were showing. It was a beautiful laugh— her trademark.

I smiled, humoring myself, and started the story again...

The cheers continued as Constantine leaned towards Nicholas. "Say something!"

Nicholas stepped forward, yet humbly. "Dear friends! It is with sincerity I must decline as the Bishop of Byzantium."

A lulling disappointment lingered in the crowd.

"Myra is my home. May the Lord bless this city, may His hand always be upon it, and upon you, fine people."

The city cheered their approval once again.

Constantine spoke up, "In honor of this great man, today, and every year hereafter, on this day, December 6th, we will celebrate Saint Nicholas Day!"

Again, screams rang out from the many levels of stone benches.

"My friends, I can only ask that you do not honor me, but in a few weeks will be the Festival of the Christ.

Keep with this celebration. Celebrate the King of kings; celebrate His love for us. Celebrate the birth of our Savior! Celebrate God! Celebrate the life of Christ!"

Nicholas waited as the crowds continued chanting.

"Sant Nic-laus! Sant-a Claus! Santa Claus!"

"I would like to ask each and every one of you to do as God has called us to do: to remember the poor, the widow, and the orphans. Share with those who have not. Relieve the oppressed and the afflicted! This is the heart of God. This is what the good Lord has called me to tell you."

The crowds had diminished, the bodies of the dead were removed from the stage, and Constantine and his mother treated a bathed Nicholas to a royal lunch in the Emperor's palace.

The room was adorned with beauty. Royal blue fabric covered the walls and tables. The plates and cups were made out of gold, adorned with rubies. Nicholas felt funny eating and drinking from something so fancy. Nonetheless, he ate, and ate, and ate.

The table was covered in the greatest choice fruits and meats, and the cups were filled with Rome's best wine.

The Emperor Constantine watched in amusement, barely touching his food.

"I was told you don't eat?" questioned the Emperor, marveling at Nicholas as he sampled everything on the table, thrusting the food in his mouth at first, but then savoring every bite.

"My fasting days are over. My prayers have been answered," Nicholas replied as he bit into a juicy peach.

"Oh. That you are free?"

"No, that the Christian church would be free from persecution in all Asia Minor." Nicholas wiped his mouth with his arm as he finished chewing and asked, "Emperor, I must know, where are the children?"

"The children?" the Emperor reacted, puzzled.

"Yes, the orphans. They were removed from the orphanages at the monasteries."

Constantine, several of his soldiers, and Saint Nicholas approached the snowy canyon on horseback, a half day's journey from Byzantium. A red tint glowed from the sun over the white powder along the east bank, rebuking the cold shadows, pushing them back with time. As the assemblage walked down into the ravine, sounds of children talking echoed among the gorge's walls. They followed the sounds for almost a half-mile.

Deep within its crevice on the west side, the echoes spilled out into the gully. A metal gate that stood about nine feet tall guarded the entry to the gap.

Constantine grimaced, looked up at the gate and rubbed his hands on it, admonishing its design. One of the Roman soldiers pulled out a universal key and opened it. One by one they entered the cave.

Nicholas barely made it inside the gate as the children swarmed him like bees to honey. Although he was very weary, he hugged and touched each and every one of them that he could.

More than a hundred children with worn clothes, dirt covered faces, and weathered skin, longed for affection from the travelers. Constantine quickly learned that his affection was desired as well from the half-starved children. Following Nicholas's lead, he dropped to his knees, allowing the kids to hug him three at a time. At first, he was nauseated by their stench, but the warmth of their friendliness overruled any smell that hindered his reciprocation. Within moments, tears flooded the Emperor's eyes.

Several of the den mothers from the different orphanages were also imprisoned with the youth, ordered to take care of them by the previous Emperor. The alternative was the same fate as the monks who fought imprisonment.

"I had no idea…" a teary eyed Constantine tried to get the words out to Nicholas. "I was away at war…"

"We should return them to the monasteries, provided they are still standing," Nicholas responded.

Constantine turned to Nicholas, a solemn look in his eyes. "Even if some of them are still standing, they are unsuitable for living at this point." The Emperor lifted his head as a sparkle shone from his eyes. "I have an idea!"

Signaling his soldiers, Constantine commanded, "Assemble everyone from the cities, tell them it's urgent, but don't tell them what it's about! Now go!"

The exodus of children led by Rome's newest Emperor was a stellar moment, and a sure sign of Rome's new rule. The hundred-something children accompanied by several soldiers, the den mothers, and the now officially titled Saint Nicholas, made their way out of the camp, through the ravine, and towards the city.

The sky peeled back her grey sheath, welcoming the sun, and warming the theatre as she glistened off the freshly fallen snow. The warmth brought many of the city's citizens, and even those from towns or cities within a day's walking distance, all curious of the new Emperor's first unscheduled surprise meeting.

By late afternoon, the seats were full, and musicians and jesters entertained the audience until the Emperor's appearance.

First, the top rows began curiously standing, "oohing" and gasping as they watched the Emperor and his men approach from a distance. The closer they came, the more noticeable they were to the lower seats in the stadium as well. Before long, most of the arena was standing, peering, and curiously eyeing the coming convoy.

The children followed the warrior to the back of the stadium and up the steps, crowding themselves on the theatre's stage and along the walls of stone and marble. The Emperor, followed by Saint Nicholas, made his way up to the front of the stage. The jesters backed away and bowed to the Emperor. The music stopped.

"Good people of Byzantium, you are probably wondering what you are doing here today! Furthermore, you are probably wondering who these children are and what they are doing here." The Emperor took a small boy by the shoulders and placed him in front of the audience, at the tip of the stage. The boy's clothes were worn and ratty, his dark hair a mess, partially covering his eyes. He was probably about nine or ten years old. "I stand before you today to ask of you in a dire matter, to not think about the cost, but to think about the benefit…"

The tall, thin, balding man with a thin mustache and beard, sitting about seven rows back on the left side, smirked, exposing his rotted teeth as he said sarcastically to the shorter, fat gentlemen sitting to his right, "What are they, slaves? Do they want us to buy the children?"

Constantine continued, "…Saint Nicholas, Bishop of Myra, the man we honored yesterday, encouraged us to reach out to the orphans, the widows, and the poor. Standing before me are more than a hundred orphans…"

"Where'd they come from?" someone yelled out from the top of the theatre.

"…These children need a home. They need love. If you truly believe the words of this man, if you want to be a part of this new, reformed Byzantium, a city moved by love and not fear, today you shall receive your opportunity. Help me change this city. I ask of you, with honor and mercy, to take these children as your own. Love them as your own. Raise them as your own. They need a family."

A man shouted from somewhere in the crowd, "What about the orphanages?"

"The orphanages no longer exist, and we don't have time to rebuild them..." Constantine spoke carefully. "An orphanage cannot give them the personal love and attention that you fine people can. Please, who is willing to foster an orphaned child, to love them, and to be loved back?"

The Emperor waited for a response. He and Saint Nicholas scanned the crowd for possible volunteers, to no avail. Constantine took a deep breath, looked to his right hand guard and received a nod.

"The government will give you incentives for taking in a child," the Emperor commanded.

"Yeah? Like what?" piped a curious doubter in the crowd.

"Lower taxes, for starters..."

The crowd hummed with applause as several volunteers stood up. Constantine looked over to Nicholas and smiled a sigh of relief before addressing the crowd again. The crowd hushed, waiting for more incentives.

"Free governmental food from the Emperor's supply."

Again, the noise level rose as the people began talking amongst themselves.

"It's just a few weeks until the Festival of the Christ. For every home that takes in a child and loves them as their own, a sign must be placed above the door on the outside of the house before the eve of the festival!

"What kind of a sign?" someone yelled.

"Something we have plenty of. Something that cannot survive without a fostering host, just as these children would not survive without you! Mistletoe! It's one of the only plants that thrive in the midst of our harsh winters, and a beautiful representation of the life these kids will live. Let it be a symbol of life and love thriving in the midst of hardships. Hang it above your door. This will signify the government of your participation, and your first inducement of gifts for the orphans and your family will be delivered. Of course, there will be an examination of potential parents."

Midgets Harry and Andy made their way down the Coliseum's top row and met up with Nicholas behind the stage. Nicholas greeted them with long, warm hugs and tears.

"We've been praying for you, Saint Nicholas!" said Harry.

"Thank you. Your prayers were felt. What are you doing here?"

Andy anxiously addressed him, "We came to find you. Sharon's ill again, and we didn't know what to do. We were here yesterday but couldn't get to you. She doesn't have much time!"

Almost all of the orphaned children were received into families throughout the region. The few that didn't became property of the government, and Constantine welcomed them into his quarters as hired servants until proper family could be found, or until the orphanages were rebuilt.

Nicholas made his way one last time down the dreary stairs and into the underground grave for the living. The guard opened death row's cell for him, by authority of the Emperor, and allowed Nicholas to gently pull his baby fir up by the roots, removing it from the soil beneath it. Nicholas exited the cell and smiled at the guard.

"This is a symbol of life in the midst of darkness. God is always growing us, even when we think we are in the midst of death."

The guard didn't say a word, but looked at Nicholas with stone cold eyes, as if he was trained to not respond to prisoners, or now ex-prisoners.

Chapter 15

Andy, Harry, and Nicholas, wasted no time traveling to the heart of the mountains, home of the dwarfs, and headquarters of a children's dreamland. The reindeer galloped, skipping from rock to rock, swiftly gliding upon the terrain in eager anticipation.

Nicholas couldn't wait to see Sharon, and pondered all the things he would say to her. He thought about his harsh nights in prison, his hope rekindled by the memories of her smell and smile. He expelled a jolly laugh at the thought of little feet running around the house, shaped like his, or perhaps like hers. Perhaps they would live in the mountains? Although a little cold, the dwarf village was a beautiful place to settle, he thought. He looked down to his precious project, the baby fir nestled safely beside him on the sled. It reminded him of her. It was life.

He then thought about the church, his call, and his reinstatement as Bishop. He realized that he had a choice. He didn't have to go back to Myra. Besides, the monastery was burned badly, and his monks were scattered. He could still serve God and not be a Bishop. Of course, he couldn't be in a church. But that wouldn't stop him from spreading the gospel or reaching out to the poor. What did *he* want? What did God want? He knew what his heart was telling him.

Andy interrupted Nicholas's warm thoughts of love. "Everyone has worked so hard! You wouldn't believe the workshop! But what are we going to do with the presents, now that the orphanages are gone?"

"You'll see! Trust me. It will be a beautiful Christmas, and now, we have the favor of the Emperor."

Nicholas succumbed to reality. He realized God's call on his life, his anointing as a Bishop, and his amazing newfound favor with the Emperor Constantine. Would he give up changing an empire for his own personal selfish love interest? Would he disappoint Christ? His heart weighed his decision heavily. He would always love Sharon, but he was a servant of the Most High God, dedicated to a life of celibacy, holiness, honor, and service. Would he be exchanging intimacy with the Father for intimacy of a lesser kind? Would God still do miracles through him? He wondered.

The orphans were spread out into different homes in the province of Byzantium and the surrounding towns. For the most part, many of the families were very welcoming. Some of the children were paired together, and many of them received baths, haircuts, and clothes right away. The new foster parents wasted no time placing mistletoe above the door, one for each child in the house, including the natural born children, to receive their governmental issued rewards.

The pair of reindeer was exhausted as they reached the small winter wonderland village. Cold clouds puffed like misty mushrooms from their nostrils. It became obvious that two reindeer alone could not handle delivering the presents across the region.

Nicholas made his way out of the sled, plummeting into the gleaming snow. It was a lot deeper and colder than before. He marveled at the reindeer's feet, having no problem keeping balance and standing atop of the thick, frosty mass. He gazed around the little white village, his eyes dreamy with delight. Red velvety cloth spiraled around columns and trees, glass balls and ribbons adorned branches, and beautiful red and white poinsettias aligned the rocky trails that led to many of the cottages.

Nicholas pet one of the reindeer as he walked past them, thinking one last time of his decision. He loved Sharon, but he could not keep her. He would cherish her friendship and their memories. He made a promise to God a long time ago, and he chose to keep his vow.

Andy led the way as Nicholas followed, snow crunching beneath their feet.

"Why red?" questioned the Saint, looking at all of the decorations.

"Think about it," Andy answered, while he waddled down the path to Sharon's house. Nicholas didn't respond. Andy stopped, turned around and offered, "Why do you wear red as a Bishop?"

Nicholas felt silly.

Andy raised an eyebrow, nodded as if to say, "*Get it now?*" and continued his path. He whispered, "We take the festival of the Christ seriously up here." He slowly opened the door to Sharon's cottage, and tiptoed into her bedroom.

Nicholas followed.

Sharon lay colorless, barely existing. Nicholas felt a pounding in his heart, not an excited pounding, but almost a crushing or a breaking. Leaning over his could-be lover, he caressed her forehead with his hand. She was warm with fever. He softly pushed her hair out of her face and knelt beside her on the bed.

"How long has she been like this?" Nicholas whispered in a hushed, bedside voice.

"Over a week."

Andy watched him, hoping, knowing that their love would heal her ailment. Nicholas took her right hand with his left, with his right hand still on her forehead, and slowly closed his eyes, bowed his head and started to pray.

It was a fresh morning, and the dwarfs greeted Nicholas with waves and smiles as he made his way to the Christmas toy workshop. Andy led the way as they entered the front of the building. Nicholas stopped, rubbing his hands along the magnificent carvings in the cherry wood doors.

Upon entering, many of the dwarfs were still working on wooden toys.

"We need to be done with everything by the end of today! Tonight's the big night!" yelled the little man with a green pointy hat and a red beard.

Andy walked Nicholas through the backside of the factory, past the row of completed toys facing the east wall, and to another door, leading to a large, dark, barn. Andy ran through the barn and opened the double doors from the other side, allowing the light to spill in. Nicholas stood there, curiously looking at the large cloth covering before him.

"Are you ready for this?"

Nicholas cocked his head and answered, "For what?"

"You'll see."

With that, Andy pulled the cloth covering off the large object to reveal an oversized red sleigh, painted with gold trim. It was shiny like a red apple and was topped with a hanging lantern in front.

"Magnificent! And it's just my size!" Nicholas chuckled.

"Exactly! And plenty of room for the presents!"

"So do you expect your reindeer to pull this thing?"

"Not two of them, but...this baby can handle eight of them."

"You've got to be kidding me," Nicholas shook his head in awed disbelief.

"Listen, if you truly want to make it through the night and cover all the territories, you're going to need all of them to reserve their strength."

"How many of them do you have?"

Andy beamed, "Eight!"

She shivered in her bed, cold sweats wetting her sheets. The great healer stood over her, checking on her one last time before preparing for his flight. He couldn't tell her of their fate. Not just yet. She was too ill and he was afraid the news would cause her to get worse.

He pondered her health and the effectiveness of his prayers. It always amazed him how God would use him to bring healing to some of the people he prayed for, but not for others. He also noted how sometimes the person would get healed the second he prayed, but others would get healed hours or days after he prayed for them. It was a mystery, but a constant reminder that ultimately God did the healing. He was just the vessel to offer prayer for God to bring that healing. "Why not now?" he asked, as he looked up to Heaven.

Bishop Nicholas put on his newest red suit, another gift made by Sharon before she got ill. It was thicker than the previous outfit, but similar in style. He fastened the thick leather black belt around his waist, holding both folds of his red wool jacket in place. He pulled the black leather boots up over his red, furry wool pants, which were a hilarious invention to him. Were they not a necessity to protect him from freezing to death, he would have worn his normal clothes; well, normal clothes for a Bishop, anyway.

He put his black mittens on and made his way to the sleigh, where Andy and another midget were preparing the reindeer. Several of the deer were restless and were bucking and fighting with the dwarfs.

"Have you ever put them all together before?" asked St. Nicholas, as he walked over to one of the restless ones and stroked its furry neck to calm it down.

"Nope! This is the first time."

"Great," the Saint said sarcastically.

The reindeer bucked and snorted, frozen smoke coming from their mouths, miniature icicles hanging from their moist noses.

"Andy, I'd really like you to come with me."

"I have to watch after my sister. I'm sorry."

Calling the reindeer by name, Saint Nicholas snapped the reins and the sled moved at a brisk pace, the blistering winds of the cold night punching him in the face. He pulled his red cap with white fur trimming a little lower on his head and ears. His thick red suit with matching white, wooly trimmed sleeves and collar kept him warm in what could normally be considered life-threatening conditions. He didn't care. He had children to think about. He was celebrating the gift of Christ by giving to those without. The anticipation fueled him.

"Whoa, ho, ho," Nicholas yelled out like a boy on a roller coaster as the reindeer flew down the frosty, white bank, dancing on the loose terrain. The ride was bumpy and unsure. Saint Nicholas reached the valley and glanced up at the moon and stars. It was a clear night and the sky displayed her majesty. As the snow thinned and the trail widened, the reindeer refused to let up, each one encouraged by the next, building upon each other's strength and enthusiasm. It was as if they knew what they were doing, and they were as just as excited about it as Nicholas was.

The Bishop reached the first village and slowed the reindeer down to a light trot. They were finally in rhythm, learning how to flow in sync with one another. The first house on the right had two mistletoe plants hanging from its doorway. The second house had one. Nicholas cautiously stopped the reindeer and reached into the back seat of the oversized red sleigh, opening the first satin sack of toys and goodies. He reached in and pulled out some candy, nuts, fabric, and wooden toys. Then, he made his way slowly over to the first house, placing the gifts beneath a tree by the front door, hoping the branches would protect the goodies from falling snow.

"One down, a hundred to go… Dear Lord, please help me."

It was almost morning. It seemed that the gift-giver covered more houses than the number of orphans from the concentration camp, but Nicholas didn't mind. He loved to bless children. The reindeer slowly approached the barn, the last few miles energized by adrenaline alone.

Saint Nicholas collapsed as he stepped down from the sleigh, sinking in the fresh white powder.

"Water!" one of the dwarfs said to another, who brought a pail over.

Nicholas sat up. "Thank you!" he exclaimed, expecting something to drink.

The little man in the yellow snowsuit walked past Nicholas and held the pail beneath the first reindeer, offering her a drink.

As he staggered across the snowy walkway and approached Sharon's door, Nicholas heard weeping from within. He softly knocked, then, slowly opened it. Harry was sitting in the front room with tears running down his face. He didn't say anything. He didn't have to.

Nicholas walked into the bedroom to find Andy sitting beside his sister, holding her lifeless hand. He didn't even notice Nicholas walking up and sitting on Sharon's other side. Nicholas tilted his head, his eyes heavy and despondent. He took Sharon's other hand and kissed it. Tears began streaming down his wind-burnt face.

Death had become a natural part of Nicholas's life. He longed for it. The very God he still served took everyone he ever loved from him. His goal was Heaven, and everyone was there except him. He thought about his parents, David, Peter, Marcus, and now Sharon, basking in the presence of Almighty God, exploring Paradise firsthand. He hungered for a taste of it. He smiled at the thought of his possible role in Sharon's salvation, but missed her touch on earth. Oh, how they could one day be together for eternity, side by side in Glory.

He rolled over in his bed, the tears catching on the chapped skin of his face. It was freezing outside, and he was numb, not by the temperature, but by the remnants of his emotions. He was accepted here. He was loved here, not because he was a Saint, but because the dwarfs knew how to love everyone with a childlike love. He belonged here, but being here without his beloved Sharon was torturous.

After resting up for a few weeks in the village, Nicholas decided to return to his ministry in Myra.

Her walls were scarred; her insides barren except the leftover rubbish charred a blackish grey. Snow had accumulated in the Myra chapel and down several of the corridors from the exposure through the missing pieces of the roof. Nicholas stood in the sanctuary as the light snow continued to fall on him. His knees met the wet chunks of shaved ice where the altar used to be as he prayed. It was still his monastery. But there were no monks to help him.

He missed Christmas. He didn't think about the orphans he delivered presents to this year. He didn't get to see their faces as they gasped their delights. He didn't even care. His heart was broken. He'd been through enough, and he was tired.

He sat in the solace of the building. Sure, it wasn't aesthetically comforting, but the stillness of the place gave him peace. Although Satan's marks were there, God's presence was still evident. It was the first time he'd been able to actually wind down, quiet his soul, and listen for the voice of God.

Hush. Quiet. Be still, he thought. No people present, no monks to take care of, no crowds, no moans from men in prison, no laughter, no animals or their funny noises, just stillness.

"This is the voice of God," he said to himself. He breathed in deeply, still on his knees. "Lord, what's your will for me now?"

Chapter 16

More than a month had passed and the Myra monastery was being transformed from the inside out. The snow had kept the majority of the townsfolk indoors. However, time brought a gentler, warmer weather and the local patrons made their way by the monastery, nestled in the heart of the city. They often gawked and gazed into the windows, trying to get a glimpse of what was making the noises from the inside, anticipating the grand opening.

The master builders, the masons, carpenters, and artists, short in stature, but with impeccable skills, offered their talent to assist Saint Nicholas in designing the most unique monastery man's ever seen. Rome itself would be jealous.

Not wanting to be seen, the dwarfs worked mainly in the evenings and rested behind closed doors during the days. Nicholas assured them they were free to be seen, but they still didn't trust the government, even though Asia Minor was now claimed a Christian province. People still had their prejudices, and the dwarfs had experienced that firsthand for many years.

Two little men sawed in the foyer, one on each side of the double ended device, keeping a steady rhythm as the blade quickly cut through the thick of the wood. Another dwarf carefully laid shades of shiny red and white tile on the floor in a circular pattern, creating a masterpiece of a design. Several of the dwarfs stood on ladders as they painted the walls and ceilings with scenes from Nicholas's life and ministry. The window frames were made out of steel and painted white. Nicholas wasn't sure he liked it, but it was definitely something to draw attention to. Another dwarf carefully trimmed designs into the many cherry wood doors.

The monastery stood three stories tall in some places, and the Bishop made his quarters on the third floor. There was a walkway from the second floor dormitories to the top of the chapel. The walkway was out in the open, and gave Nicholas a place to talk to God at night as he stared out at the stars, or a place to preach from to those in the city streets.

A host of ships returned to Myra for trade as the Saint was constantly ordering new material for the monastery; exotic woods, precious metals, tools, rare spices, etc. He more than compensated the sailors for their trouble. Many of the merchants offered the money back in return for Nicholas's blessing on their lives. Their faith paid off, as their businesses would double whenever the Saint prayed for them. Myra was a booming city, and Nicholas's generosity was helping it grow.

Many wondered where the man of God, vowed to a life of poverty, got the money to build such a beautiful place. Some assumed it was a gift. Others believed it was a divine blessing from God. Still several skeptics accused him of taking money from the poor or making a deal with the government.

Nicholas visited his parents' tomb for the last time as he removed the last of the money from behind the loose brick in the tomb wall. Luckily, his very wealthy father had taken him up to the catacombs when he was just eleven years old and showed him where the family's fortune was hidden, protected from confiscation by Rome. Neither Nicholas nor his parents knew that they would be dead the following year, but God did. His father bought the apartment-sized cathedral-like tomb because he was given a deal too good to pass up, and considered it a brilliant place to protect costly belongings in times of war. The graves faced the east in a rocky cave on a high cliff off the coast of Myra, overlooking the Mediterranean Sea, the perfect spot to see Jesus coming in all his glory. His parents imagined they would be one of the first souls to join him at his return, at least that's what the salesman told them when they bought their rock-cut tomb, sized for two.

As the seasons unfolded, and the summer's sun erased any remnants of the harsh winter, word of Myra's magnificent monastery and its famous Bishop quickly spread. He was appointed on the Council of Nicaea by Constantine the Great, gaining him even more popularity in the Christian community among leaders outside of his region. It was the first ecumenical council of the Christian Church in history, and Constantine hoped for Christianity to become the religion of the world.

Leaders from all over the world, including kings and queens, came to visit the famous monastery and offered presents to the Saint. He stowed the gifts under his fir, the very wee fir he began growing in death's dungeon. She grew to almost six feet, and graced the corner of the chapel. She was dressed in glass balls and ribbons, modeled after the village of his miniature friends. However, the secret of their designers and where they came from stayed with Nicholas. He would often give away the ornaments to the leaders who visited, in exchange for helping the poor. His fellow monks thought it was a little odd to have a tree inside a church and monastery, but they had so much respect for their world-famous Bishop that they didn't mind his eccentricities.

The small, beat-up monastery of Myra was now a remodeled, state-of-the-art, world famous tourist trap. The new monks didn't seem to mind, although they were a little curious about the stories of some of the paintings. The dwarfs disappeared months before the new recruit of monks arrived in Myra, and Nicholas refused to tell them whom the paintings resembled. One of the most admired paintings was that of Nicholas and Marcus giving food to the poor, found in the chapel ceiling. However, some have argued that it's Nicholas and his best friend, Peter, getting free food from the market to give to the orphans, telling a story a few decades old. Mostly, they questioned about the painting on the outside wall of the bishop-like man with high arched eyebrows, a scowl look, a frowning face, who appeared angry at the world. They couldn't figure out why this man was being honored, or who he was, or why he was so angry. Some speculated it was Cardinal St. Michaels in his undergarments. Others thought perhaps it was Peter, personal friend of Jesus, the rock of the New Testament.

Speaking of the Cardinal, God has a way of doing things and making wrongs right. Diocletian's men demolished to the ground the compromising monastery at Patara. Only the outline of a foundation was left, with weeds fighting for space where the dining hall used to be. The town itself was damaged by a severe hurricane in the Fall, destroying homes, businesses, and porting docks. Merchants and sailors never returned, but took their business to Myra. Eventually Patara became a forgotten wasteland.

Epilogue

Decades had passed. Nicholas stood in the center of the sanctuary. The red, white, and turquoise tile designs were beginning to wear, and the inside paintings of him, Marcus, and Peter were starting to fade from the sun. His baby fir was now a grown, mature young adult. She was pushing ten feet, much larger than her intended growth. She was planted outside the monastery, full and rich green, still adorned with ribbons, lace, and glass-blown balls. Several of her younger offspring grew inside the monastery and sanctuary's walls, also ornamented in beautiful apparel.

He pulled on his growing white beard, glanced around the room, and smiled at the promising young monks before him.

"Tomorrow, I'll make my annual trip to the mountains." Bishop Nicholas inhaled heavily, changing the course of what he was going to say.

"Every year I make this trip, and it amazes me how the trees all die, the plants die, Fall's colored leaves are gone, and a thick white blanket of snow covers their death..." Nicholas paused. "Think about it for a minute. How can we relate this to our lives in Christ? What is Christ trying to say to us? What happens after that thick, white, purifying blanket covers death? The sun reappears and it brings life again."

Nicholas tottered on his cane and looked into the eyes of each and every soul in the room. He lifted up a portion of the Bible and began to translate from the Gospel of John; "Listen to me... I tell you so. Unless a kernel of wheat falls from the flower onto the ground and dies, it continues to be only a single seed. But if and when it dies, it produces many seeds, producing much more harvest.

The man who loves his life will lose it... The man who hates his life in this world will save it for eternity."

As the first snow of the season fell, the monks watched Nicholas travel towards the snow-capped peaks one last time. He never returned and was never seen again.

Over time, the wild tales of a dwarf village in the mountains, reindeer that could fly, and a Saint gift-giver became no more than a myth and a legend to his monks and the townsfolk of Myra. He never talked about it to protect the desired anonymity of his friends.

He supposedly took the month off every year to get away from those wanting to honor him in December. He humbly declined to be recognized for what God was doing through him. Others thought he was visiting the grave of his lover, still mourning over her death. Still some speculated he was going up the mountain to hear from God, much like Moses did in the Old Testament of the Bible. Although no one knew for sure, some still believed that Saint Nicholas, the amazing secret gift–giver, was still alive, living with the dwarfs, dispersing presents to children every year on Christmas Eve.

The year following his disappearance, many Christians throughout Asia Minor and most parts of the Roman-owned eastern world placed a fir or a prayer tree in their homes on December 6, through the Festival of the Christ, decorated with ribbons and ornaments to give honor to the most influential saint of their time. They would write out prayers on mini scrolls and tie them to the tree with ribbons. Little did they know that the morning of the Festival of the Christ, every boy and girl who placed a tree in their home that year would find gifts miraculously placed under it and in stockings hung by the fireplace.

The mysterious news spread throughout the world, leading to an explosion of homes celebrating Christmas with prayer trees. As the economy prospered, gift giving at Christmas became contagious, and families began exchanging gifts with one another in honor of Christ's birth, the true reason for the festival.

Several years later, Roman soldiers took a number of the monks from Myra to Constantinople for questioning. The powerful city of Byzantium was appropriately renamed in honor of the great Emperor Constantine. The government stopped incentives by the 2nd year of the exodus of orphans, and they were curious about the continued miraculous gifts to the children, oppressed, and the poor, primarily on Christmas Eve. The monks were questioned about the tree, the presents, and Saint Nicholas. It was assumed that there was no way that their former Bishop could be providing all the presents to homes by himself, and the government assumed that the monks were participating in his outreach. They also wanted to find a way to tax the creators of such gifts.

The monks assumed that Saint Nicholas was dead and that there were dwarfs involved in the gift distribution, theorizing that dwarfs truly did exist, but would never tell that to Rome. Of course, several of the monks still heard the faint voice of their previous Bishop in the night, once a year, yelling out to his reindeer by name. One monk who was deathly ill one Christmas Eve said the saint visited him during the night in his dreams. Many of his friends thought he was just delirious from fever as he shared comical details about a furry red and white snow suit the Bishop appeared to be wearing. He said the saint encouraged him to continue looking out for the poor. Then, he prayed for the young monk, vanishing into thin air, and the next morning he awoke healed.

After carefully investigating the Myra Monastery for one year and discovering the monks' lack of activity on the eve of the Festival of the Christ, Rome questioned the newest Bishop of Myra again.

"How is this happening? How can one man bring presents to so many homes in one night?"

"It's called faith," smiled the new Bishop. "It's the miracle of Christmas."

A body for Saint Nicholas was never found. However, almost a decade later, friends of the Bishop held a funeral for him. An empty casket was buried outside his church in Myra, with one of his favorite Scriptures etched into the tombstone.

Stand up for those who cannot
Stand up for themselves,
Fight for the rights of those who are
destitute.
Speak up and be honest and fair;
defend the rights of the poor, hungry,
and needy.

Proverbs 31:8-9

Almost a century went by and the city of Constantinople claimed ownership of Nicholas's body. Puzzled by the continuation of gifts appearing in homes all over the world, the latest Emperor had the casket opened, only to discover the casket empty except one of Nicholas's canes and a white substance called manna growing from it.

I looked down to see Gabby's head leaning against my chest. Her eyes were shut, and she was breathing hard, probably in a deep sleep, dreaming about candy canes, hot chocolate, and Barbie dolls. Our company had long gone, and the remnant smells of cinnamon lingered in the air. I glanced over to Makayla, who routinely brings a pillow out and falls asleep on it in front of the fireplace. She was so little and adorable; her tiny body barely stretching the length of the small fireplace. We called her our peanut, and rightly so. At the age of four, she was the height and weight of a two year old. It seemed that every other generation since the beginning of time our family produced at least one short, small framed peanut, and sometimes more than one.

Mommy had taken Elisha to bed an hour earlier, and left me alone with my two sleepy girls, our bodies still glowing by the few leftover embers in the fireplace.

I gazed into the fire, full of anticipation for the morning. She hissed a lullaby through the searing wood chips on her altar.

I enjoyed sharing our Christmas story with the children, as it's been passed down in our family from generation to generation, much like the peanut gene. However, the girls always seem to fall asleep before I ever get to finish it. Perhaps next year I'll be able to tell them the true and complete ending. Perhaps then the girls will hear about their uncle Andy from generations earlier, and how we were almost related to the great Saint Nicholas. Perhaps.

The End

About the author:

Matthew Eldridge lives with his lovely wife and three beautiful daughters in metro Atlanta. Besides writing stories, Matthew is passionate about songwriting and playing music. He has recorded a number of albums, and plays a variety of instruments.

What can you expect in the future? With a zealous fervor for Peretti and DEKkER novels, you can expect something along those lines. Matthew has a passion for historical fiction, but is also a child at heart – leading him to write suspense novels based on true historical events or characters, with a hint of fantasy involved. His next novel, *Whiter Than Snow* – is the real snow white story, based on the true life of Margarete von Waldeck, lover of Prince Phillip II of Spain. Don't let the title fool you – this is no child's fairy tale. Matthew's short story series, *The Fear Box, The Sin Cage, and The Suicide* should be available by the time this is in print.

Matthew Eldridge is available for speaking engagements, book signings, and radio interviews. Please contact him .

Feedback is encouraged!

meldridge@cheerful.com

770-364-3990

Thank you for purchasing this book. I hope that you enjoyed it. There are more to come so make sure you stop by my website at www.mattheweldridge.net

~Matthew